THE
INVERTED
CAVERN

By

Todd A. Fonseca

RIDAN

A Ridan Publication
www.ridanpublishing.com
www.thetimecavern.com

Copyright © 2011 by Todd A. Fonseca
Cover Art by Michael J. Sullivan
Layout Design and Editing by Robin Sullivan

ISBN: 978-1-937475-50-5
PRINTED IN THE UNITED STATES

First Printing: November 2011

for
Justin Anthony Fonseca
with love

Your enthusiasm and excitement
for this volume kept me going
along with the frequently asked question:
"Is it done yet?"

PRAISE FOR THE TIME CAVERN

"Todd Fonseca's Time Cavern is filled with adventure, mysteries, and life lessons all crafted into a charming tale. I loved the little fun facts woven throughout the story, which made it an enjoyable read even for someone my age. I highly recommend this fantastic book…well done, sir."
— Michael J. Sullivan, author of *The Riyria Revelations*

"Charming is the only word I can think of to describe this book. The Amish element, the two cute kids, their families, the old barn, and, of course, what they discover in the woods is a compelling blend."
— Sandy Nathan, author of *Numenon*

"The mystery of The Time Cavern is clever, well-thought out, nicely researched in its details, and leaves me wanting more. I would love to read more of this story, so I hope a sequel will be forthcoming. Very well-written & highly recommended to readers of all ages!"
— Rai Aren, author of *Secret of the Sands*

"While reading The Time Cavern I was totally transported back to my childhood when I was an avid reader of both the Hardy Boys mystery series and, yes, even the Nancy Drew mysteries. Those books were great back then and Fonseca has captured the essence of what made those books great and has brought that essence forward in time for today's young readers."
— Gary V. Tenuta, author of *The Ezekiel Code*

"Todd A. Fonseca's "The Time Cavern" is a fantastic read for children and adults alike."
— J.R. Reardon, author of *Confidential Communications*

Books by Todd Fonesca

Aaron & Jake Time Travel Series

The Time Cavern (The first adventure)

The Inverted Cavern (The second adventure)

CONTENTS

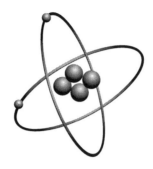

Contents (cont)

THE
INVERTED
CAVERN

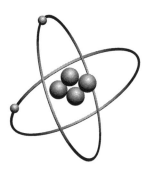

Chapter 1

ONE GIANT LEAP FOR AARON

Aaron crept along the invisible bridge surrounded by the violently vibrating water. While he had done this before, it felt different this time. Every fiber in his body told him something was not quite right, and over the years he had learned to trust those feelings.

There should be no reason for his apprehension. The last time he had jumped into the vortex, he had not even known what would happen. This time should be easier. He already knew what lay beyond the portal.

Aaron had made sure that he and his friend Jake had thought everything through. They had discussed possible problems and created backup plans. He was sure they had not missed anything.

I guess it's just natural to be nervous, he tried to reason with himself. *After all, it's not every day that you travel through time.*

As he neared the vortex, it appeared as though time was slowing down. The light shimmering on the water looked like a movie played at three-quarters speed. The vents surrounding the enormous pool produced loud vibrating tones singing in full chorus—belting out their harmonies and causing the water to dance in response. Above him, the starry sky was projected on the dome of the cavern. The red circle at the apex indicated his destination time—exactly one hundred years into the past.

A huge drop of water formed at the end of the discharge tube and then fell ever so slowly—as if the laws of physics had been altered. When it finally reached the large pool, it kicked off another set of rippling waves. Light from some unknown source danced on the water, reflecting the replica of the night sky that illustrated distant stars and galaxies.

Aaron shifted his gaze to Jake who stood at the controls. Her face free of the concern and angst it had shown on previous occasions. After uncovering irrefutable proof that she and Jake would travel through time she had become a true believer. The look on her face reflected her confidence and her faith now appeared unshakeable.

He took another step forward, and it seemed as if his leg had slowed unnaturally. It blurred and left a streak from where it started to where it landed. Even more disturbing, it also appeared semi-transparent.

That didn't happen the first time, he thought. The sick feeling in the pit of his stomach intensified. *Maybe something is wrong.*

He and Jake had placed the control levers in the exact same positions as when they had sent the Amish boy back home—and yet Aaron did not remember seeing the slowing of the waves, the blurring of body parts. When he had watched the other Aaron enter the vortex, however, he and Jake had been fifty yards from where he is now. From that distance, it was difficult to see anything near the vortex very well.

Aaron raised his hand. It too had that same dreamy, blurred appearance, as if he was only partially in the cavern. Watching his limbs move so strangely reminded him of those pictures taken at night of cars driving down a street. The automobile's image started and ended at two places and showed a blur of the car's body streaking between them.

Weird, he thought. *Why didn't this happen before?*

The strange blurring was not the only difference. The vibrations seemed more intense this time as well. The water around the platform splashed toward him trying to invade the one remaining calm area of the pool.

In just two more steps he would be at the outer edge of the vortex. This was the point of no return. Here, time and space swirled violently together as if the fabric of reality was being torn. The power of the vortex pulled, drawing him in. Ironically, the intensity of the vibrations and deafening sound of the vents actually diminished as he approached the middle.

Aaron's heart raced, pounding blood through his veins, and a cold sweat broke out over his skin. *Something's not right,* he thought. The certainty he had usually felt regarding the cavern had vanished, replaced by a desire to flee. He forced himself to calm down by taking deep cleansing breaths—he needed to think clearly.

This is not a time to freak out. Nothing bad is going to happen. Jake knows exactly what to do.

He looked at the platform again. Even from this distance and through the violent dimensional disturbance, he could see Jake's supportive, smiling face. Seeing her, his fear was quelled and he determined to enter the vortex with vigor.

All right, he thought. *Let's do this with style.*

Remembering his summer track lessons, he took a few steps back, then rushed forward with long fast strides and leapt as if he were competing at the long jump. Flying through the air, a smirk plastered across his face, he gave Jake two thumbs up and looked in her direction.

What he saw chilled his bones.

Jake was no longer on the platform. Instead, she was racing down the path, pointing and shouting at him. Even from this distance, he saw the look of terror on her face. She was frantic and he had no idea why. Whatever the problem was, she was too late. He was already in midair directly in the center of the vortex. The pull of the time field had him and he slowly sank. Before the horizon of the quivering pool consumed him, the last thing Aaron saw was Jake's face contorted by her scream—and yet he heard nothing.

Chapter 2
EARLIER THAT WEEK

Aaron and Jake stared speechlessly at what they had uncovered. "It worked," Jake finally said with disbelief. "I mean it really worked! The Amish boy went back in time just like you said he would."

She ran her fingers over the intricately carved wooden box that had been handed down through generations of Amish. They had been given instructions indicating when, and to whom, they should give the box to. To Jake and Aaron's great surprise, they had been the designated recipients. What they had found inside led them to buried treasure, literally. Behind the old barn, buried under a large willow tree, was a crate full of helium bottles and a diary—the Amish boy's diary.

"Do you know what this means?" he asked.

"Yeah, we can finally tell everyone what's going on!"

"No," he said defiantly. "We still can't tell anyone."

"Why?" Jake stood and brushed dirt from her knees. "This is amazing." She pointed at the crate. "We've actually found a time machine and have proof now. We know how to work it. Imagine where we can go. What we can do. This could change everything!"

He replied calmly, "Exactly."

Jake furrowed her brow and Aaron knew that her pride was keeping her from asking what he meant by that.

"The thing is," he explained, "with a time machine, everything could change—the present, the past—all of it."

"Here," he said, handing her the diary. "take this." He pulled the crate out of the ground and filled the hole with the dirt. "We need to hide the diary so no one finds it." He checked his work. "Good enough for now," he said. "We can make it better later. Let's hide all this stuff in the barn."

Aaron lifted the crate with a jerk. He had expected it to be heavier than it actually was and wondered if the helium inside helped with the weight. "If others learn about the time cavern, who knows what could happen. What if someone went back and changed history either on purpose or by accident?"

"How could they change history?" Jake argued. "It's history and has already happened."

"I don't know," he said. "But maybe they could change the way things are now."

They entered the barn and Aaron set the crate down.

"So where are we hiding this?" Jake asked.

Aaron pointed. "I was thinking we could put it there, next to the chest."

"Hmm, how heavy is it?"

"Not very, it looks heavier than it is."

"That's good, but it's big, and the ladder is not very sturdy. I don't think we can carry it up there."

"You're right," he said. "But how did the old gear chest get up there? Come to think of it, the hole in the loft isn't big enough to fit much of anything."

Jake flashed him a smirk.

"What?"

"I feel better now," she said, smiling.

"What do you mean? Are you making fun of me?"

Jake giggled. "A little."

What the heck? he thought with annoyance. "Would you care to share why?"

"It's just that you usually have a plan or answer for everything. It makes me feel like I'm an idiot sometimes. But now I feel better."

"Glad I could help. Are you saying I'm an idiot?"

"No more so than when I don't get something as fast as you do. It just goes to show that we each have our own smarts."

Whatever, Aaron thought. *And what the heck does "each have our own smarts" mean? Who talks that way?*

"All right, so I give up. What's so obvious?"

"The hayloft!" Jake replied. "How do you think all that hay gets up there? Those bales certainly wouldn't fit through that hole."

She's right, he thought. *A bale of hay is much bigger than the chest or the crate. What am I missing?*

"Stuff is loaded through the hayloft's *doors*." She drew out the last word. "Ever notice how big they are and what is above them?"

Aaron ran outside and understood immediately. *How had I missed that before?*

Above the doors, near the top of the barn, was a pulley. After some rummaging, they found an old but sturdy rope. Jake was always braver when it came to heights so she did the hard part. Aaron watched as she leaned out of the hayloft doors to loop the rope through the pulley. Her outstretched fingers missed, barely. Sticking out her tongue in concentration, she flailed about trying to grab the pulley. Aaron realized what she was about to do when she repositioned her foot close to the edge and took a grip with one hand on the door's frame while balancing her weight on one leg.

"No, Jake, don't!" he yelled.

But it was too late. She pushed up on to her tiptoe, leaned way out, and somehow managed to thread the rope perfectly before pulling herself back inside the barn.

"What?" she yelled back.

"Never mind," he replied, his heart racing.

Jake fed him down the rope, and he tied it around the crate. She raised it slowly and then dragged it to its proper place next to the chest.

Aaron joined her and looked out the loft doors, admiring the sunset's final orange hues that were giving way to the blue-gray of the night sky.

"So, explain to me what you meant about changing the past," Jake asked.

"Honestly," Aaron said, "I'm too tired to get into it now, and besides you've got to get home. It's getting late. Let's talk about it tomorrow."

Chapter 3
SODA JERKS

They had agreed to meet at a place called, *Soda Jerks* to talk about what to do next. Having never ridden his bike to town before, the trip turned out to be farther than Aaron had expected. The morning sun of late fall radiated off the dusty brown dirt road as beads of sweat stung his eyes. While navigating a sea of jarring potholes, he raised his butt off the bike's seat and used his legs as shock absorbers.

Arriving at Main Street was a welcome relief. He settled onto his seat again, and coasted down the small hill that led into town. He rode past his favorite *junk store*, which was home to an impressive assortment of electronic parts, many of which had been slated for future science or robotic projects. To the right of that was the candy store, and next to that stood the salon where he had used a tanning bed's UV light to make a faded, hundred-year-old diary page legible once more.

The complete diary, along with a variety of other items, went everywhere he did—just in case. The assortment rattled about in his well-worn backpack.

When he had told Jake why he took the stuff everywhere she had asked, "In case of what?"

"I don't know," he had told her. "That's exactly the point. You never know what might happen or what you might need to get yourself out of trouble!"

An old two-story stone and brick building at the intersection of two streets was home to *Soda Jerks*. The stonework was ornately carved and inscribed above the door in large gothic letters was the word: APOTHECARY. Aaron wondered what that meant and made a mental note to find out later. Floor-to-ceiling windows were protected by large red and white striped awnings, and a sign in the same colors read:

SODA JERKS

Aaron rode onto the sidewalk and parked his bike in the waiting stand. He did not bother with a lock. No one locked anything here. When Aaron opened the door, a small bell rang overhead. He paused a moment to let his eyes adjust from the sunny outdoors.

"Over here," Jake shouted. She sat on a chrome bar stool with a red leather seat. He took the one next to her, plopping his backpack on the bar.

"It's getting bigger," Jake said, poking her finger at the ever-expanding rip at the bottom of his pack.

"Yeah," he replied. "I should probably tighten the shoulder straps. When I ride my bike it sometimes rubs on the back tire."

"Why don't you get a new one?" Jake asked.

Aaron stared at her in shock, as if she had asked him to cut off his left arm. "You're kidding, right?"

"Sorry," she said, and spun on her stool. "Isn't this place cool? It's like going back in time."

"Don't say that," he said. "Someone might hear us."

"You've got to be kidding. No one has any idea about the cavern."

Aaron relaxed and took a moment to look around. The entire shop was a throwback to early ice cream parlors. Ornately stamped tin covered the ceiling. An enormous mirror bordered in a dark wood hung behind the bar and framed the back wall. Black-and-white tiles checkered the floor and wire frame chairs with heart-shaped backs surrounded the tables.

Jake noticed him looking at them. "You know what those are called?"

"Ah, chairs," he responded.

"Duh, but what kind?"

"The kind you sit in?"

She laughed. "No, they're called sweetheart chairs because of the heart shape. My parents said this was where boys and girls used to meet on dates in the old days."

"Interesting…oh my gosh!" he said, pointing at the end of the room.

"What?"

"Is that a jukebox?"

"Yeah," Jake said. "My dad always pops in a few coins when we come here. I haven't recognized any songs he plays, but my folks seem to enjoy them. It's the real deal all right. Full of old-time records—no CDs or MP3s."

Aaron nodded his head. "Yeah, this place is pretty cool."

From behind the counter, an older gentleman wearing a white uniform came over and rested his hands on the polished marble countertop. "Hi Jake. Who's your friend?"

"This is Aaron. His family lives in the farm next to ours."

"Nice to meet you," the man said, offering his hand. "My name's Frank."

Aaron shook his hand and read the man's nametag, "Soda Jerk."

"Excuse me sir," Aaron said, more politely than either of his parents would have ever imagined. "This store is named *Soda Jerks* and I noticed your name tag says just about the same thing."

The man smiled and nodded. "You want to know what a soda jerk is, eh?"

"Right!"

Aaron saw Jake listening intently as well. *Maybe she doesn't know what it means either.*

"You see these here?" the man said, grabbing one of the gooseneck spouts that rose from the marble countertop. When I pull this large lever on top, soda water comes spraying out. I use it when making good ol' fashion ice cream sodas. There aren't too many places that have real soda spouts anymore, but back when these types of places were popular they used to call guys who worked in them soda jerks because of the jerking motion we use to put the soda water into the glass. I thought it would be a good name for the place."

"Cool," Aaron said. "What do you think, Jake? If that is their specialty, I think we've got to have a couple of ice cream sodas—my treat."

"Great. I'll have cherry!"

"And for you?" the man asked.

"I'm sticking with chocolate," Aaron replied.

They watched the man grab two tall glasses stacked behind the counter. He added flavored syrup to each and scoops of ice cream. Finally the soda water was added. Using long spoons, he mixed the content of each glasses and handed them over along with napkins.

"Enjoy, kids. Next time you come in, you should try my other specialty."

"What's that?" Aaron asked.

"Ice cream sundaes!" Jake said before the man could answer.

Aaron took the long spoon and straw and savored what he was sure would be the best ice cream treat he had ever had.

"Wow, this is good!" he said.

"I know," Jake agreed. "We don't come here very often because my mom says that it would make us all as big as our house."

Aaron laughed. "I can't believe how good this is," he said, taking a moment between bites. "I almost feel guilty."

"Funny you should say that," Frank said, wiping the counter. "That's one of the stories behind how the ice cream sundae got its name."

Aaron and Jake looked at one another. "What do you mean?"

"Well I heard that in some midwestern states, laws were created that prohibited the sale of ice cream sodas on Sunday, the day of the Lord, because they were so good some people considered them to be sinful. So soda shops started selling ice cream sodas without the soda water, leaving just the ice cream and syrup. Since they sold them on Sundays, they called it an ice cream sundae."

Aaron and Jake gaped at him. "Is that true?" Aaron asked.

"Well it's hard to know for sure, but it's a popular story. Guess we'll never know. Too bad we can't go back in time and find out."

Aaron paused mid-slurp and Jake let out a little strangled choking sound.

"You okay?" Frank asked.

"Sure," Jake quickly replied. "Just got a little too much."

Aaron hopped off his stool and grabbed his soda and backpack. "C'mon," he said. "Let's go to one of those booths." Frank looked at him curiously and Aaron explained, "My legs are starting to fall asleep from dangling off the stool."

Jake followed him to a booth near the jukebox. "What was that all about?" she asked.

Aaron slid into the seat, unzipped the pack, and pulled out the diary. "Well if we're going to talk about this, we need to be out of earshot. Fortunately there aren't too many people in here, but at the counter it would be impossible to talk with Frank there. Don't get me wrong, he's a great guy but we've got work to do."

"Okay," Jake said. She crossed the room, filled a pair of small Dixie cups with water, and returned to the table. "Here," she said, giving him one. "I'm thirsty. It happens every time I have ice cream."

Aaron took the cup and drank as Jake reached out and took the diary. "Okay, here I go," she said while carefully opening it. "I bet you were up late reading. Is there a really good part? I'll bet—"

"What are you doing!" Aaron said, grabbing it back. Frank turned toward them and Aaron shrugged.

"What's with you?" Jake whispered, leaning forward. "You've had it all night. It's only fair that I get a chance to try and catch up." She tried to take the book back but Aaron stopped her.

"You don't understand," he explained in a similar whisper. "I haven't read it at all."

Jake's eyes opened wide. "Like I believe that! All the answers to secrets about the cavern, a journal of our own writings and travels, probably an explanation for exactly how the cavern works, and you expect me to believe you haven't read it yet? Right! Hand it over AJ."

Aaron hated when she called him by his initials. "No," he replied firmly. He was not kidding.

"But why?" she asked. "We finally have the answers, or probably do, and they're right there. Don't you want to know?"

"Of course," he said, replacing the diary in his backpack. "But I started thinking about our conversation at the barn."

"About the hay bales and the loft doors?"

"No, before that," he said frowning. "Remember what I said about the dangers of changing history?"

"I remember you started to say something, but never finished."

"Right. Okay, so let's imagine if someone went back in time, say fifty years ago, and went to the barn loft and removed or destroyed the diary page I found."

"Okay," Jake said, waiting for more.

Aaron shook his head. "Think it through. If they destroyed the diary page, I couldn't have found it when we moved in."

"I get it," Jake said, nodding. "Then we wouldn't have found the cavern. I guess we wouldn't even know it was there."

"Exactly, worse yet, we might not have become friends." He played with the napkin dispenser by twirling it on the table. "That diary page brought us together, if you think about it."

Jake smiled. "That's nice to say. But you don't know that. Maybe something else would have brought us together."

Aaron nodded. "You may be right. But I think you get where I'm going."

"I kind of see. But that's not what happened, is it?"

"What do you mean?" he said.

"I mean no one took the diary page."

"Obviously," he said.

"I know it's obvious. What I'm trying to say is that if someone had done something like that we would never know the difference. I mean we wouldn't remember the experience of the cavern or anything. We'd have totally different memories. Who knows, maybe someone did take the page originally, and someone else put it back so this could happen. Maybe someone needs to know about the cavern as a time machine to put everything right—assuming this is right, I guess."

Aaron considered the logic. "I suppose it's possible. I just think it's better if no one else knows for now. It's also the reason we can't look at the diary."

"I'm still not sure I get it," she said.

"The stuff that's in the diary, the things we haven't done but are going to do, they're written there. As you said, it has the answers. The problem is, if we know what is going to happen, then we could change it."

"But why would we want to change it?"

"I don't know if we would. But knowing will make a difference. What if something bad happens or someone got hurt. We would be tempted to try to change things, right?"

Jake tapped her fingers on the table. "Maybe we should change it if we can prevent someone from getting hurt."

"You may be right, but it will still change everything, and maybe worse things will happen. It's impossible to know."

He could see her thinking about it. "I have a question then," she said. "You already know about this—I mean the problems of knowing too much about what's going to happen, right?"

"Yeah," Aaron said wondering where she was headed.

"And the stuff in the diary talks about things that are going to happen in the future—our future."

"Yes," he said. "What are you getting at?"

"In the future, you still know these concerns about sharing and knowing too much information, yet you must have told the Amish boy to bury the diary so we can have it now."

Hmm, she has a point.

"Clearly," she said confidently. "You wanted us to have the diary with its information so we could use it. You must have already weighed the consequences of having us know versus not knowing."

"Great," Aaron replied, throwing his hands up. "Now I've got to figure out why I'd do such a thing. Especially since my future self knew we would have this conversation and I didn't leave any instructions for what to do."

"Maybe you did. Maybe it's in the diary." She grabbed at his backpack.

"No!" Aaron slapped his hands on top of it. "It would have been something different, like the note the Amish boy left us in the carved box. I would have been clear what to do with the diary. My instincts tell me we're supposed to have the diary, but we are not supposed to use it—at least not yet."

"Hmm, I suppose. That sounds a lot like you anyway."

"What do you mean by that?" he asked.

"Well you never give the answer. You're always trying to make me figure it out."

"I thought that was a good thing," he said, finishing his water.

"Mostly it is, but it depends if you are trying to prove how smart you are. Then it's frustrating."

"You're right," he replied. "I'm pretty frustrated now myself. Yet the future me knows the answer and has decided not to share it."

Aaron took out a notebook and opened to a he had written. "Well I'm not going to rack my brain about it anymore. I'll know when the time is right to use it. Let's talk about what we should do for our first trip back in time."

Jake pushed the glasses aside. "Okay, what were you thinking?"

"Well we were able to send the Amish boy back with these settings exactly as we wanted. I'm thinking we shouldn't get too fancy. We could use the same settings to go back and see him. You know, use a known point in time. Hopefully he'll be right near the tree. Then I'll set the levers to the moon setting, jump in, and wait there. After you see the vortex close, you could wait five minutes or so and restart the process with that same setting." He showed her a notebook in which a diagram of the lever's locations was drawn and labeled, *moon setting*. "Then I'll jump out and we'll know it was a success. Simple."

"I agree," she said without hesitation.

"You do?" he questioned.

Jake never agrees, he thought. *Where is her concern? The talk about how dangerous this is? Why isn't she asking about the things that could go wrong?*

"Okay, what did you do with Jake? You agreed too easily. C'mon, what's going on?"

Jake laughed. "Nothing's going on. I have faith that's all."

"Why all of a sudden?" Aaron asked. It's not like—"

"Hey you kids," Frank said from behind the counter. "Need anything else?"

They were so involved in their conversation that they had forgotten they had finished everything.

"No, thanks," Aaron replied. "Just talking."

"Okay, let me know if you need anything."

"Maybe we should leave," Jake said.

"No," Aaron replied. "We'll be fine. No one can hear us over here. This is a good spot. And since you're so agreeable, we'll be done soon!"

"Thanks for making it sound like I argue about everything. *Nice*!" She hesitated. "I'm *so agreeable*, as you put it, because of the diary. Everything you said would happen, did happen, and the diary proves we will have adventures in time. That means it has to work out. Maybe that was why you sent the diary forward, to give me confidence."

"Maybe," he said. "What about the levers, you think you can handle them okay?"

"No problem! I can't believe you're the one who's worried. After all, what's the worst thing that can happen?"

Chapter 4
ONE GIANT NIGHTMARE FOR JAKE

Jake watched from her perch on the platform as Aaron approached the vortex. For the first time since they had discovered the time cavern, she felt free of anxiety. Finding the completed diary, and having seen Aaron's and *her own* handwriting, had convinced her that the future would work out. She had seen the proof with her own eyes.

True, she did not know all the details, but that was all right. The information was in the diary and Aaron would not have used it to go into the future unless he was supposed to. When the time was right he would use it on his journey back.

She daydreamed about what it would be like to go back in time—to see the differences. What would it look like? What did people wear? What did they do? What about school? She was excited to go, to be a part of—

She shook out of her reverie as Aaron stopped and looked toward her. Even from the expansive distance of the cavern, she saw his apprehension. *That's strange*, she thought. *He's never worried about anything before.* She beamed a glowing smile to him, which did the trick. He smiled back.

What's he doing now?

Jake watched as Aaron took a few paces back from the vortex.

Oh no, the diary!

The backpack's splitting seam widened, and she saw the lower corner of the diary hanging out. Jake bolted down the path waving her arms.

Aaron did not see her. He was in his own world.

She shouted, but it was futile. The cavern's chorus blared over her feeble cries.

Aaron took off, bounding toward the vortex.

What's he doing!

With each step, the diary slipped through the ever-enlarging seam. She would be too late.

Suspended above the swirling vortex, he turned, flashed a smile, and thrust two thumbs up as she raced on in horror. The diary dropped out and fell into the shimmering pool just before Aaron disappeared from sight.

She reached the water's edge and stepped out onto the invisible bridge surrounded by the violent, trembling water. Immediately, the vents started to close, and Jake shot a look toward the platform to see what had happened. Had someone shut off the levers? After a moment of confusion, she realized that the water feeding the large pool had run out. The echoing sounds faded, the star map on the ceiling disappeared, and an eerie calm settled over the water. Jake continued on. As she neared where the vortex had been, she looked down and found the water was now flat as glass, reflecting her own image.

Without a second thought, she thrust her hand into the water, which sent out concentric waves. She did not know why, but she had expected the water to be cold—instead it was as warm as bathwater. She splayed her fingers and searched for the bottom. For a moment, she wondered if there was one. Perhaps it was bottomless? Would she be willing to jump in or even dive underneath? What would she find? A huge drain?

Her hand touched down. The water was only a foot deep and the bottom was extremely smooth. Searching for the diary was like trying to find a light switch in a darkened room.

Nothing.

Maybe it fell farther away from the bridge.

Balancing precariously, Jake extended her arm, and as she was about to give up, her middle finger brushed something. Straining, she stretched farther. Her fingers grabbed the flap, and as she withdrew it from the water, she knew she had found it.

"Oh my gosh!"

She ran back to the water's edge. Carefully, she set down the book…the book with their stories…the book they had taken care to bury and hide for a century…the book with the directions on how to operate the cavern.

"Oh my gosh, oh my gosh." The ink bled out from the pages.

The diary was ruined, and Aaron was gone.

Chapter 5

AFTER THE LEAP

Pain came from everywhere.

His back ached and his leg throbbed. It took a while to realize his leg was *under* his back! Aaron tried to move.

Pain!

Flashes of white light shot into his brain even though his eyes were closed.

Another flash erupted, but he had not moved—then another. Were the flashes caused by the pain?

Where was he?

What had happened?

A loud crack exploded and the ground rumbled. His body tensed.

Wetness fell onto his face. It was cool and more drops hit him as the thunder crashed once more. *Thunder and lightning*, he thought. *I must be outside.*

Aaron risked opening his eyes.

Darkness. Deep darkness interrupted by occasional lightning revealed he was in a forest.

The patter of rain drops increased followed by a blinding flash—

more lighting.

His leg, he needed to move it from under his back. Holding his breath, Aaron squeezed his eyes tight and counted to three. He rolled to his left, reached under his back, and grabbed his leg. Pain pierced his body. He screamed as he released his leg from its pinned position. Blowing quick breaths, Aaron buried his face in the twigs littering the forest floor.

The rain came down harder and the tree's canopy no longer provided much protection. His shirt and pants grew heavy as water soaked his clothes, chilling his body. Aaron shook his head furiously, fighting hard to stay conscious. Aaron turned his face skyward and brushed aside his hair. The pain was unbearable.

What am I going to do? What went wrong?

His mind tried to process what had happened. Recent memories from the cavern replayed in his mind.

Right, he thought. *The cavern…Jake. I was going back in time. We planned for everything…*Then he remembered her screaming as he jumped. What was that about? Where was he? What had happened?

He worked through the pain, pushing it to the back of his mind as best he could and struggled to remember entering the vortex.

He had expected to see a long wormhole-like tube of swirling light. *I've seen too many science fiction movies,* he thought. But the truth was it had not been anything like that. At least he did not remember it that way. What he remembered was a bit more bizarre.

As he entered the time field, everything had faded to white like an overexposed picture. The pounding vibrations of the cavern faded, and his body felt numb. Something tore at him from the inside, ripping apart the very core of his being. *Maybe my soul,* he thought. Whatever it was, it came loose and drifted apart from his physical self.

It was out. *He* was out. Aaron saw himself, or what was his body.

THE INVERTED CAVERN

Was it a dream? An umbilical cord connected his drifting self to his physical body like an oxygen tether used by a deep sea diver. He should have been afraid, but felt calm, instead. His body was just a shell. What made him, what truly made him, was separate from his physical self.

Then, piece by piece, starting from his toes and the tips of his fingers, tiny flashes of yellow light erupted. After each flash, that section of his body disappeared. Starting slowly the pace began to increase. It seemed as if Aaron was being taken apart cell by cell and replaced by light. Soon his entire body was gone, replaced by one large pulsating yellow light connected to the umbilical cord.

Acceleration.

Aaron felt like he was being pulled along. The light wrenched him through whiteness, then darkness, and into whiteness again. Then his body re-formed piece by piece.

He blinked and found that he was back in his body and falling… falling through darkness.

Then came the impact! And the pain.

I never should have jumped into the vortex like an idiot.

A noise got Aaron's attention. Someone was coming.

I'm saved!

"Over here, Michael." Aaron heard a young masculine voice. "I heard the scream come from this direction."

"Samuel," another voice replied, "this is crazy. We can't see anything in this rain. Let's come back in the morning!"

The anxiety in their voices kept Aaron from calling out. He heard the thrashing of underbrush and saw two small flickering lights approaching. *Some type of lanterns*, Aaron thought. They were close. He could almost see who they were. The lights stopped and one figure turned to face the other.

"Michael, Sarah said this was the place. The place where *it* happened."

"Unnatural is what it is, Samuel. I refuse to believe it."

Samuel lifted the lantern to illuminate the face of his companion. Even in the dark Aaron recognized the beard and hat. These men were Amish.

Samuel poked his finger at Michael's chest. "That's the point. We've got to find this thing and…" His sentence trailed off. Both men and Aaron heard the snap of a tree branch.

"Over there! It came from over there."

They pointed their lanterns in his direction. "Come, let's go," Samuel shouted. As they closed in on Aaron's position, lightning struck just a few yards away. New sensations of pain surged throughout his body as electric energy fried his nerves.

He welcomed the blackness as unconsciousness overcame him.

Chapter 6
AN "OLD" FRIEND

H ere, drink this."
A cup was pressed against his bottom lip. A gentle hand caressed the back of his neck, tilting his head forward. Liquid flowed into his mouth. His throat protested, and he started to choke but then he managed to swallow. Warmth flowed down his gullet, radiating outward. Aaron felt better—much better.

Memories flashed in and out like a slide show ... lanterns ... the Amish men ... lightning ... unconsciousness ... arms around him ... being lifted ... pain and screaming—his screaming—unconsciousness again ... moving ... his right arm draped around another's neck ... being carried and dragged ... trees. He remembered a lot of trees and bushes ... and all the while there was the smell ... yes, the smell ... something burning ... scorched meat perhaps ... or was it wood? Smoked wood? What was that smell? Then, there was a booming sound but not thunder. He still heard the rain, but he no longer felt it falling on him.

"Can you hear me?" A voice asked. He knew the voice, remembered the accent.

An "Old" Friend

"Yes," Aaron replied, opening his eyes. A cool blue hue surrounded him. Two large branches and some wrapped cloth formed a make-shift splint to brace his leg. Broken. He was in some type of corridor or cave. A moment later he began to recognize his surroundings. The Amish boy, wearing his crisscrossed, black suspendered pants and holding a cup in his hands, sat next to Aaron.

"It's you!" Aaron said in relief. "How did you find me?"

The boy stood over him. "How is the pain?"

Aaron winced while testing his leg. "Better."

The Amish boy started to pace, his brow furrowed.

"I don't understand," the boy said. "Why are you here? This is not your time? Why did you come?"

Aaron thought he heard anger in the boy's voice. "The carved box you sent me and Jake led us to where the helium was buried. It showed us the way."

The boy stopped pacing. "I do not know what you are talking about. What box? I did not send you a box. I do not understand. I do not understand! How could I send you anything?" He resumed his pacing. "You can't be here. You can not!"

What was going on? Why was the boy freaking out? This was not what Aaron had expected. Everything was all messed up—the journey through the vortex, his leg, and now the Amish boy.

"Calm down," Aaron said. "How long have you been back?"

"I returned a couple of weeks ago. It worked as you said. But Sarah, she was gone. When I came out of the tree, she was no longer waiting for me. I should have never gone into the cavern," he said, more to himself than to Aaron. "But see, it has gone wrong now. It is all bad." The boy choked back a sob.

"Slow down," Aaron said, gingerly propping himself on his elbows and grimacing at the pain. "What's all wrong? What's going on?"

THE INVERTED CAVERN

The boy took a deep breath. "After I came back and found Sarah gone, I had no idea how long I had been away. I was not certain I had come back to my time, but there was no way to know. The tree, the forest, everything looked the same in my time as it did in yours." The boy stopped, kneeled, and massaged his knuckles. Aaron reached out and touched him on the wrist.

"It's okay," Aaron reassured him. "We'll figure it out and fix it. Tell me what happened?"

"I ran straight home. After leaving the forest and crossing the creek to our property, I saw the barn in the distance…our barn…my family's barn. It was new, just like the day we built it. I knew then that I was back in my time, but I still didn't know how long I'd been away." The boy wiped his brow with the back of his forearm. "As I approached the barn I heard pounding, and I looked inside. My father was at his bench working on a horse saddle. He stopped in mid- hammer swing, as if he knew someone was behind him. Then he asked where I had been. He said he had been looking for me.

"It was then I realized that I'd returned on the same day that I'd left, although hours later," the boy explained. "My father was none the wiser about what I had done or where I had been. I told him that Sarah and I had been playing in the forest and we lost track of time. It was not quite a lie of course," he added with a shrug. "But it was not the entire truth." The boy held his head low.

"For the next two weeks, I was busy and had no time to see Sarah and tell her I was okay. Until today that is." He rubbed his hands hard to work out the guilt. "I went to Sarah's farm earlier this evening, and I found her sewing clothes on their front porch. When she saw me, her eyes got as round as saucers. She dropped the sewing, shot off her swing, and clamped both hands over her mouth to stifle a scream. 'Calm down Sarah,' I said to her. 'I am all right, everything is fine.' I glanced around to see if anyone had witnessed her unusual behavior.

"Seeing no one nearby, we walked to her backyard and kept a safe distance from the house so we would not be overheard. Given her state, I did not want to say anything about being stuck in time and going to the future. I wanted to reassure her that I was fine and that she would never have to go back to the tree again." Pausing in the middle of his story, the boy shook his head.

"But she just gawked at me and explained that when I hadn't returned she thought I had been missing for weeks. She was frightened and finally confided to her brother, Samuel, about what we had found. He thought she was crazy and threatened to inform her father. She begged and pleaded for him to find the tree so that she could prove her story. He told her to stay home, and he took his friend Michael to look for it."

The Amish boy stared Aaron straight in the eyes. "I went out right away to find them. I wanted to keep them from finding the tree, but then you arrived...

"I was planning to tell them I had been just playing a joke on Sarah and that there was no time cavern. But if they found you, and saw your clothing and backpack...I would not be able to explain that away. But luck was on our side. Just as they were about to find you, lightning struck a nearby tree, and they ran off. I fixed your leg and carried you here."

What a mess, Aaron thought. *This can't be what was supposed to happen.* "Maybe I should have read the diary and avoided this whole thing," he mumbled to himself.

"What?"

"Nothing," he replied. "I should have known better..."

"I don't understand."

"It doesn't matter." Aaron realized they were inside the tree, and that the entrance was closed. *How?* he wondered. Jake and he had always opened and closed the entrance from the outside. *How is it possible?* That was yet another mystery, but one that would have to wait. With everything screwed up and his leg in such bad shape, he needed to get home. He had no idea how he would explain his broken leg to his folks. Maybe Jake could help. Perhaps they would tell part of the truth. They could explain that they had been climbing trees, and he had fallen out. That could work, and it was mostly the truth.

"Listen," Aaron said, "I think the best thing to do is to get me back to my time. That way, there is no evidence of me to confuse your situation, and I can get some help for my leg."

The boy considered the plan. "It is fine for you, but what about Samuel? He's sure to come back. How do I prevent him from finding this place?"

"Easy," Aaron said matter-of-factly. "I think you should show Samuel the tree."

"What?" the boy exclaimed. "That would only make it worse!"

"Trust me," Aaron said. "Here's what you should do…"

Chapter 7
JAKE AND THE MOON

"Calm down, just calm down," Jake repeated. "We talked about what to do in an emergency. Come on Jake pull it together."

Closing her eyes and taking a long calming breath, she relaxed. She put down the dripping diary and grabbed the bucket, filling it with water.

All I have to do is turn on the cavern at the moon setting, and Aaron will be there.

She knew from her experience with the Amish boy that traveling forward in time was possible. There were just two keys to success: the moon setting could be used to suspend the time traveler, and then a person in the future could set them free. When using the moon setting, one entered a strange world of time rings surrounding an old tree atop a hill. There, time was suspended.

The idea of time rings *around* the tree intrigued her as she thought back to when she was at school. "Take a look class," her Earth Science teacher had said when showing them a cross-section from a fifty-some-year-old tree. "You can see a series of circles starting at the very middle of the tree, each one larger than the next. These concentric rings represent the annual bark growth." Her teacher had gone on to explain that by counting the rings, you could tell the age of the tree. Each ring equaled one year. The outer bark was from the current year's growth. The next inside ring was from the previous year. With each smaller ring, one traveled another year back in time. Scientists called it Dendrochronology—tree ring dating. Her teacher also explained that by studying the size of the ring, one could learn about the environment—a thick ring meant a good growing season with plenty of water, a thin ring indicated a more challenging year.

I guess it only makes sense that a time cavern should be inside a tree. In many ways trees hold the secrets of time within themselves.

Like the Amish boy, Aaron had planned to use the moon setting. When he was finished with his visit to the past, he would enter the vortex and let it close, suspending him in time until someone opened the portal in the future. That was Jake's job.

Her hands trembled as she poured the water, splashing a good amount and missing the receiving pipe. The destruction of the diary was unsettling. The diary had been the thing that gave her confidence about what they were doing. It was the evidence that proved with certainty that there was a future where both she and Aaron had traveled through time, learned the secrets of the cavern, and documented their findings. And now it was gone; destroyed by the very cavern whose secrets it revealed.

It's almost like the cavern doesn't want us to have it…

She shook her head. *That's dumb. Aaron is fine. Whether he stayed an hour or a month makes no difference. As soon as I turn on the cavern, he'll be back. Together, we can figure out what to do about the diary.*

The first large opaque drops fell from the discharge tube to the cavern's pool, and the ceiling shimmered with light. Jake engaged the primary lever, and the vents and water once more transformed the cavern's ceiling into the night sky. She adjusted the levers, maneuvering the moon into the targeting area. Aaron had made it look easy. Doing it herself, was another matter. Jake did not find using the levers to be intuitive. They actually worked the opposite way than she thought they should. On several occasions just as she had the moon about to reach the apex, it ended up flying off in the wrong direction. Twice she lost complete control, and the moon disappeared from the horizon. After that she decided to stop trying to position it herself and just placed the levers in the positions Aaron had drawn for her.

It worked.

The red targeting ring brightened as it locked on.

"Yes!"

Stepping back and looking past the platform into the vast cavern, she saw the time vortex forming at the pool's center. Now all she needed to do was wait for Aaron to climb out.

Nothing.

Impatiently she placed her hands on her hips and tapped her foot.

Where is he?

After a while she checked her watch. Five minutes had passed since she had opened the vortex. Looking up she confirmed she had in fact targeted the moon. She tugged on each lever verifying its position. Jake looked over at the wet and ruined diary laying near the pool and sighed. She tried not to think about it and checked the settings once more.

Seven minutes…still nothing.

I've got to go down there, she thought. *I've got to see if he's trapped. Maybe he's hurt. Maybe he can't climb out. Maybe he's shouting at me for help, but I can't hear him.*

Another minute passed. Leaving the platform's perch, she descended to the cavern floor, the vibrations growing in intensity with each step.

As she stepped onto the water, the turbulent waves quickly overcame the small ripples made by her shoes. Another step. Would she see the tree in the portal? Would Aaron be there?

The water swirled and time warped a few feet ahead. As she neared the portal, her fear escalated. Jake knelt and crawled forward on all fours. Nearing the event horizon, she flattened down to her stomach, pulling herself forward. Her clothes became soaked clear through to her underwear. Undaunted, she reached the edge and peered down.

It was there—the tree! Elation filled her. She had done it! This was the correct setting! But where was Aaron?

She yelled, "Aaron!"

Dread filled her.

It's no use, she thought. *There's no way he can hear me. What do I do?* Frustration almost brought her to tears. *He has to be there,* she thought. *It's what they planned. There must be a reason he isn't coming out.*

Jake dared not think of the possibilities. If he was not there, he would not be coming back. The only way forward in time was through the moon setting. And if he was not there now, he would not be there in the future.

She rocked back and forth knowing what she had to do. Aaron was there, and he needed help. *I can't believe this,* she thought.

Jake Carlson was going in.

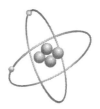

Chapter 8
TRAPPED

Aaron winced with each step as the Amish boy helped him down the winding path deeper into the tree toward the cavern's entrance.

"How are you doing?" the boy asked.

Aaron nodded, keeping his focus forward. "Fine, fine, let's just get there."

The path terminated in the antechamber to the cavern. On the far wall hung the watchful eye of the helium symbol, with its celestial-looking neutron and two orbiting electrons. To his left, the nearby wall of cubby holes was filled with small bottles.

"Okay, those would have made life a lot easier," he mumbled, remembering his and Jake's adventures getting helium in their time.

"What do you mean?" the boy asked.

"Never mind," Aaron said. "It doesn't matter now. Maybe at some point I can tell you the story, but I think we should get me home now so that I can have my leg fixed. Jake and I will have to regroup and try to understand what went wrong." Even as he said this, Aaron thought about the diary, safe in his backpack. It likely held the answers, but he resisted the urge to use it. There was no telling what the consequences would be of knowing too much.

"Here," the boy said, "prop yourself against the wall while I open the cavern." He left Aaron for a moment, took a container from its resting place, and connected its spray tube to the receiving nub in the wall. *A Perfect fit*, Aaron thought as the boy injected the contents.

The helium symbol pulsated, enlarging as the electrons raced, their orbit widening, engulfing first the wall then the entire ceiling and floor. The neutron in the middle gave way to a circular portal opening to reveal a long tube-shaped tunnel.

Using the Amish boy once more for support, Aaron limped his way down the passageway to the massive cavern awaiting them. As they arrived at the control platform, Aaron once again wondered about the mysterious cavern. How had it been made? Who made it? When was it made? What caused the light? *Maybe luminescent bacteria*, he thought, remembering a fellow student's science fair project about glow-in-the-dark organisms that lived on fish.

"Are you ready?" the boy asked, and Aaron realized his young Amish friend had already retrieved and filled a bucket of water from the pool below.

"Go ahead."

Though his leg still throbbed in pain, being in the cavern energized him. He hopped to the main control and pulled the lever that opened the tonal vents. The sounds enveloped the cavern, building to an angry symphony. The resonance pounded him to his core, and the pain in his leg intensified.

Aaron looked at the Amish boy and smiled, hiding his discomfort. "Target the moon!"

The moon rose on the distant horizon of the cavern. Slowly, it settled at the cavern's apex.

"Okay," the boy yelled. "What next?"

"Here, help me," Aaron shouted. "I have to trap myself in time like you did. Jake will set me free in the future."

Aaron explained the plan by yelling above the noise. "Any other questions? There's no way we'll be able to hear one another once we are down there."

His friend shook his head. Aaron thought the boy was probably happy to see him leave. Grasping the boy's shoulder, he gave a squeeze in a silent good-bye.

Aaron looked toward the pool and noticed something. "The vortex!" he exclaimed. "Where is it?" In the pool below, where the time vortex normally formed, nothing was there—just water.

"I don't understand," the boy said.

Aaron checked everything he could think of. Looking up, he confirmed the moon's location. "This should work," he murmured. His mind raced, trying to understand why the vortex had not formed. It always had before. He thought back to when he had entered the portal the last time, and how something had felt wrong.

Was it the water? Had it already run out and the portal was now closed?

Nope. Drops kept falling, the vents belted out their harmonious tones. The portal should be there!

"Maybe it's there, but we can't see it," Aaron yelled to the boy. "Race down and take a closer look."

The boy nodded and left.

Aaron watched him walk across the water and approach the area where the vortex should be. The boy plunged his arm into the water. Nothing. The boy shook his head.

How could it be? Aaron thought, motioning for the Amish boy to return.

"Let's try another setting!" Aaron shouted over the dizzying noise.

"Go back and refill the water. We'll target some other stars and see what happens." The Amish boy ran down once more. Aaron was amazed at his friend's stamina. Quickly the pipe was refilled and the boy returned to the control panel.

Moving the levers, the moon left the targeting circle and was replaced by a nearby star. Once locked on, the time vortex appeared.

This is so odd, Aaron thought. *Why is it working for the stars but not the moon?*

"Let's try another star."

"Okay!"

As the first star moved out of position, the vortex disappeared and reappeared when a different star locked in. Strange. Everything seems to be working perfectly. *Maybe there was simply a glitch when we first positioned the moon.* He signaled for the Amish boy to target the moon.

Aaron's anxiety grew as he watched the moon approach the target. The red ring pulsed, locking on. The Amish boy shook his head.

The vortex did not reform.

Aaron pulled the lever shutting off the cavern.

"I didn't want to do this, but I don't think we have any other choice." He unzipped his backpack and removed items he had brought for the journey—a notebook, compass, snack…he rummaged around and became concerned. He started feverishly tearing through the pack.

"What are you looking for?"

"The diary," Aaron said. "Your diary…our diary…"

The boy looked puzzled. "My diary is in my room."

"Right," Aaron said.

The Amish boy looked as if he wanted to ask a question but couldn't quite figure out what it was.

"It's complicated," Aaron added. "Let's just say that I think the answer to our problem might be in the diary."

"If that is true, and you've had the diary this entire time, why didn't we look at it sooner?"

"You know, you and Jake are a lot alike. Lots of—" Aaron never finished his thought. He pulled items out in earnest, and then finally turned the bag upside down, shaking out the remaining contents. "Oh, no!" he cried.

"What?" the boy asked. "What is it?"

"It's gone," Aaron replied, searching the pile. "It's not here. I can't find it." He thrust his hand in the various pockets, and when it emerged from the ripped seam, his face froze.

The hole!

"It must have fallen out," he said, scanning the platform and the pathway for the diary. "We'll have to retrace our steps. Maybe it fell out when I arrived in the forest or when you carried me to the tree. We have to find that diary or I'll never get home!"

Chapter 9
THE SEARCH

T hat was a close call!" Jake went cold just thinking about how she had almost made a huge mistake. As she had been about to enter the vortex, it closed because the water had run out. She still could not believe she had almost trapped herself inside time, just like the Amish boy. What would she have done then? She would have been trapped in the moon setting with no one to set her free. Jake shivered.

I've got to think and stay focused. No stupid mistakes! One thing about Aaron, he thought through everything. He always had a plan. She used to make fun of his preparations; now she appreciated what he did.

She used her watch to time another test run. When the cavern's vents closed and the vortex disappeared she recorded the reading in her pocket notebook: *10 minutes, 48 seconds.*

Listed above that entry was a similar reading: *11 minutes, 4 seconds.*

For a third time she repeated the test. The final entry—exactly eleven minutes.

Okay, she thought, reviewing the data. Another column of numbers was titled: Time from platform to vortex.

It takes me about three minutes to get from here to the water vortex, and it stays open for about then minutes. That means I've got seven minutes to get in and out before it closes.

Then, in big bold letters, she wrote:

TARGET TIME: 5 MINUTES!!

She grabbed the pile of vines she had collected from the forest and twisted them together to form a makeshift rope. Testing its strength, she pulled each section to ensure it would hold her weight. Jake was not going to take any chances and get trapped. In the twine at about every foot or so, she tied a knotted loop to create foot and handholds. She fastened the end of the twine near the pool's edge to one of the vent hoods.

After filling the bucket to the brim, she walked slowly to the platform. Her shoulder and arm muscles tightened as she fought to keep the bucket as steady as possible. She did not want to spill any. When she got to the levers, she paused.

It was time.

She set two countdown timers on her digital watch; the first to five minutes—the second to seven. She would have to enter the vortex, find Aaron, and get both of them out before the first alarm sounded. The second timer, she did not want to think about—it was her last signal; the time when the vortex would close. She would either be out in seven minutes or trapped forever.

Her face flushed as adrenaline rushed through her veins.

Can't over think it now. Once you start, you've just got to go.

She stretched her neck in an attempt to relax and focus.

Giddy up!

Jake dumped the water into the pipe, and raced to the vortex which was already forming in the pool below. Reaching the water she started the timers, grabbed the vine, raced to the portal, and launched herself, clinging to the rope for dear life.

She saw the tree as she jumped into the portal, but instead of getting tangled and falling through the branches, she suddenly found herself standing on the ground. It was odd—one minute she was dangling from her precarious rope through a hole in the sky, and the next she was down, safe and sound. The massive tree towered over her, and above it the rope hung through the portal. For a moment she wondered what would happen if the portal closed. Would the rope get severed at the point where it entered the portal? Would half of it fall to the ground and the other half remain in the cavern? Perhaps the portion held between both worlds would disappear.

I don't have time for this!

She glanced at her watch:

4:05

Oh man, I've already used up a minute!

"Aaaarron!" she shouted. "Aaaarron!"

She checked behind the tree and looked into the branches above. If Aaron was here, he was not close by. She needed to make her way to the concentric translucent time fences. It was difficult to concentrate on the task at hand. Even though Aaron had described this place, the bizarre yet strangely beautiful scene was hard to ignore. She descended the hill to the first time fence and saw images of different people and places. These were scenes from the past. Things that had already happened, played out in front of her like a historical movie. She ran along the first fence that circled the hill. The images and even the sounds changed from one area of the world to another. Her trip around the hill was also a trip around the world. Feeling she was moving farther away from where she needed to be, she doubled back to the Midwest.

She approached the fence with caution, recalling how Aaron had said he had walked right through a screen. When she touched the image, it distorted. Her hand passed through, and the screen broke into multiple narrow, vertically-spaced images. Testing a theory, she placed both her hands back to back, then inserted them into the screen. She pushed them apart, as if she were opening closed elevator doors. The smaller vertical images compressed and radiated out from either side.

She repeated the gesture several times. On a hunch, she tried the opposite direction—splitting the screen from top to bottom. This worked as well except instead of traveling across the screen, this moved the strips from top to bottom. Experimenting in this way was fascinating, but as she tried another, she noticed the remaining time on her watch.

1:15

"Oh, no!" she exclaimed. "Only one minute left!" She plunged her body through the image fence to explore farther. She shouted for Aaron, running through one fence after another. After a while she stopped to catch her breath. Jake felt the same way she had on that day several months ago when she had been trapped in a corn field by row after row of identical stalks, uncertain of which way to go to get out. The image fences were tall, at least six feet high and she was not sure how to get back.

Think Jake, she scolded. *Hold it together, all I need to do is run back up the hill.*

0:38

THE INVERTED CAVERN

There was no longer time to search for Aaron. She would have to come back later, and she ran uphill passing through fence after fence. Reaching the tree's base, she climbed. It was exactly like the one in her forest, and she knew the fastest way to the top. Nearing the halfway point, the five minute timer went off. Startled, Jake's foot slipped off a limb mid-reach. The grip with her other hand gave way and she fell. Limbs, leaves, and bark flew by. She grabbed at whatever she could to stop her descent, scraping her arms and legs as she fell. Digging into the trunk with her hands, a finger nail ripped off and she yelled as she crashed to the ground.

There was no time to even check her watch—she had to get out!

Remounting the tree, she climbed, faster this time. For a moment, her mind flashed back to when she and Aaron had raced down the tree. It was then that they had discovered the hidden panel. She wondered, *if this tree is identical to the one in the forest...*

Jake climbed fast but focused on not falling. She saw her make shift rope.

"Got you!" she said, grasping the twine.

Then the second timer went off.

Chapter 10

SAMUEL

The midmorning sun beat down relentless in a cloudless sky. Samuel adjusted his hat, thankful for the shade it provided. Already, his shirt clung tight as sweat dripped freely down his back. Lifting the ax, he brought it expertly through the wood, splitting the log in one blow. He knew he was strong and few could match his skill.

His mind drifted back to Sarah. The storm had cut short his and Michael's search. When they had returned Sarah had begged him not to go back. Why she had changed her mind he did not know, but he was now more curious than ever.

While placing another log on top of a stump, Samuel spotted the boy—Sarah's friend. *Not missing after all,* he thought. He set the head of the ax down and leaned on the handle for balance, watching as the boy approached. Lost in thought, the other boy seemed unaware that anyone was spying on him. Sarah's friend suddenly stopped, then counted on each finger—as if ticking off items he wanted to remember—then he nodded and continued forward.

Hearing the sound of their front door open, Samuel watched as Sarah stepped out onto the porch. She ran to the boy, and after a quick side-to-side glance, she leaned toward her friend. Samuel chuckled. Although he could not hear what they were saying, watching them told him quite a bit. Her hands and arms waved and her volume rose. There was no doubt that she was upset. In his entire life Samuel could not remember seeing his sister as upset as she had been over the last few days.

Odd, he thought.

The boy took the scolding with slumped shoulders, but when she was finished, he countered. Grand gestures of his own explained his side of the story. Sarah's body language began to change. At first her arms were crossed, but with time, she unlocked them. Samuel was intrigued and wondered what had happened.

As if on cue, both stopped talking and looked in his direction. Samuel felt a sudden unease. For a moment, he stood frozen in their gaze then decided to go back to work, lifting the ax. His concentration faltered and the blade grazed the log, sending it flying off the stump. Samuel recovered and was thankful that he had not hurt himself. When bending to retrieve the log for a second try, he saw Sarah and the boy walk behind the house near the forest.

What are they doing?

Samuel eyed the pile of stacked logs. It would be a long day. This was only the first of many chores.

The two continued unabated toward the tree line. Sarah looked back hesitantly, her face filled with fear. The boy grabbed her arm and she quickly turned. The two continued their march.

That's enough. Samuel thought, and left the ax and wood. He decided to follow, but kept his distance. Once they entered the forest, Samuel jogged and closed the gap. He did not want to lose them in the dense trees. He maneuvered through the brush carefully so as to not expose his presence.

"This way," he heard the boy say. Checking where they were, Samuel thought it was a completely different direction than the one Sarah had told him about previously. He had to admit, however, everything looked much different during the day than it did at night, especially during a rain storm.

"Here we are," the boy said.

Samuel crept closer, advancing only when they spoke to hide the sound of his movement. Spying from behind a thick tree, the backs of his sister and the boy faced him. Beyond them, two massive tree trunks snaked and intertwined, reaching for the sky with their heavy canopies. Their rough bark was deeply crevassed like the leathered face of an ancient man. The two trunks became one at about ten feet or so off the ground. Below that, a large inverted V-shaped cavern stood black in the trees' shadows.

"It is your turn this time," the boy said to Sarah.

She shook her head.

"You said you would go," he prodded. "It's only fair."

Her shoulders drooped, and the boy nodded.

"I will go and retrieve the ancient wish stone."

What is a wish stone? Samuel thought.

Sarah's friend walked forward, leaving Sarah outside the tree. The boy entered the cavern, and the darkness shielded him. A moment later, he brought forward a smooth, flat rock and handed it to Sarah. "With this rock you control the sky and stars." He placed her hand upon the rock, and traced her palm with a small white stone. "The ancient twin trees provide the entrance through which you must walk. With your hand placed inside this outline, wish for the time you want to visit. I will wait for your return."

Sarah hesitated, silently pleading to her friend. Her eyes darted in Samuel's direction, and he ducked behind the tree, hiding.

Did she see me? A moment later he released the breath he had been holding, since the two did not seem to notice him.

"It is time," he heard the boy say. Samuel waited before looking to make sure he would not be discovered. When he did dare to peek, he saw that the boy was alone. Sarah was gone. Time slowed. Samuel suddenly noticed how quiet the forest was. No animal sounds. No rustling of leaves. Quiet. Calm. Disturbing. And no sounds came from inside the tree. What was going on? An eternity passed, while the boy stood like a statue. Samuel felt a millipede crawling up his leg, and tried to ignore it. It did not take long for the sensation to become overwhelming, just as he reached to scratch it away, Sarah's friend yelled.

Startled, Samuel struggled to keep control of his bladder. He was about to charge from his hiding place but refrained. He watched as the boy ran around the two trees screaming and knocking on their trunks. Over and over he chanted, "time, time, time, time." On his third trip around, Sarah emerged from the crevice.

Her friend fell silent.

Sarah shook her head. "You are very loud!"

"I wanted you to know your time was up. It's my turn."

"I don't want to play this game anymore. Maybe we could go climb trees or something?" Sarah asked.

The boy shrugged. "I guess. I think I saw a good one near where we came in."

Samuel watched as they walked off.

A game, he thought. *This was a game?*

Anger grew as he made his way home. He did not have time for children's games! His sister had not pulled a stunt like this before. Come to think of it, she had never acted so upset. Was she purposefully trying to trick him? Kicking at the underbrush as he walked, he struck a hard object and launched it forward. Sunlight reflected off of its surface before the item descended into a bush. Curious as to what it might be, Samuel raced forward, keeping his eyes locked on where it had landed. Reaching through thorny branches, he grasped the object and pulled it from its vined cage. Samuel did not know what it was. The object was long, tubular, and made from a silvery metal. What he did know was that there was a lot more to Sarah's story than just some silly game.

Chapter 11
THE CLOSE CALL

Jake's forearms twitched as her muscles ached from exertion. Water soaked her hair and cooled her body as she lay on the invisible bridge staring up at the cavern's ceiling.

That was close…too close.

The final drop fell as she exited the portal, the time field ejected her as the vortex closed. How long would she have been trapped there…weeks…months…years…longer? Her thoughts trailed off as they were too disturbing to consider.

She propped herself up on her elbows and looked behind her. The center of the pool was calm, and no remnants of the vortex remained. As she rubbed her fingers through her tangled hair, she felt her fear subside.

Aaron, she thought. *He wasn't there.* At least he was not close to the tree. But he had to be. Even if he had spent days or months living in the past, the plan was for him to get back using the moon setting. So if he was not there, it meant he never came back—ever. That thought was too much to consider. No, something else was going on.

The answer lay near the edge of the pool—the soaked diary.

Unfortunately, it was ruined and useless.

Wait a minute…Maybe there is a way. Aaron had read the faded diary page by using a tanning bed's UV light. Was there a way to save a water-soaked book?

A memory triggered. A few years back the harsh winter froze their pipes at home. One burst and drenched the cabinets under the sink in the kitchen. Hundreds of her mother's family recipes that had been kept for generations became completely waterlogged. They had been stored in a three ring binder and Jake thought they were destroyed forever. But her mother had saved them. Taking the binder, her mom opened it with care and made sure not to rip any of the heavy, delicate pages. She separated groups of ten or so pages from each other and placed paper towels in between. Once the towels were saturated, she replaced them.

Later Jake helped her mom finish drying the pages with a fan, keeping them flat by placing books on top. It had worked—mostly. Though some pages were beyond repair, many were saved.

Jake dashed home; there was precious little time to salvage anything from the diary. Searching the front hall closet, she found a stash of paper towels. Jake grabbed a roll and scrambled up the stairs before her parents could ask any questions. With the diary on her desk, she interweaved the paper towels. After the last page, she closed the book and saw the water already beginning to bleed away.

She waited for the paper towels to fill with water, then replaced them. While she waited for them to soak once more, she thought about how to keep the portal open longer. Five, or even seven minutes, was not nearly long enough to explore the area around the tree when the cavern was set to the moon setting. Jake wanted to make sure she could search far and wide for Aaron in case the diary did not hold the answers.

Okay, she thought, plopping down on her giant pink beanbag chair.

THE INVERTED CAVERN

She opened her notebook, pen in hand—*time to brainstorm. Water keeps the portal open. I either need more water or a way to make the water last longer.*

She started a list:

<u>Ways to get more water</u>
- Use a bigger bucket
- Use more than one bucket
- Keep pouring water in the pipe until it won't take anymore
- Have someone else pour water in while I'm in the vortex

Jake thought about the last one. Who could she trust? Not to mention that Aaron would go nuts; he did not want anyone else to know about the cavern. *But these are desperate times, aren't they?* Another person could ensure that the portal stayed open, besides, she almost got trapped herself today. This realization made up her mind, and names of kids from school went through her head. After considering each she came to the conclusion that she could not trust any of them. She did not know any of them well enough. The fact remained that Aaron was her best friend, and in many ways her only friend. No, there could be no one else. Whatever the answer, it would have to come from her alone.

It's brainstorming, she told herself. *Now's not the time to judge!* Unfortunately, the ideas dried up. *What about some crazy stuff?*

- Run a hose from the house to the cavern. *Ha—I like that one!*

- Take a bunch of ice cubes and place them in the pipe so they melt slowly and the water lasts longer. *Nice, that's really good. Look at me. Aaron would be impressed! Of course I don't know if the ice would melt fast enough…Argh stop judging…*

THE CLOSE CALL

How to make the water last longer
- Ice cube idea from above
- Maybe water isn't the only thing that works—what about other things like dry ice?
- Maybe water plus ice cubes?

Jake thought about the shower heads her father had installed a few months ago. He called them "low flow"—which meant they used less water over the same time. When she asked how they worked, he said the size and shape of the shower head's holes made the water droplets smaller. *Maybe a similar gizmo in the cavern would help.*

Reviewing the list, she realized none of the ideas were ideal. Of course, the perfect solution would be a nonstop water supply—then the portal would never close. She decided to cross off any idea that did not provide a continuous flow. After working the entire list, two items remained as potential "perfect" solutions. The first was having an extra person; they could continually feed the water into the tube. The second was running a hose from her house to the cavern.

Tapping the eraser end of the pencil on her notebook, Jake shook her head. While no one from school made any sense, perhaps there was someone else. Parents? No, not yet. One of Aaron's brothers? TJ was smart, but still too young to trust with such an important job. No, there was not anyone else. Jake drew a line through that option.

One left—running a hose from the house—she laughed out loud. *Right,* she thought. *Like I could find enough hose to reach the cavern! Ha!* She started crossing it out then hesitated. *Too bad there isn't a water spigot closer to the cavern.* Then it hit her. There was not a spigot, but there was a lot of water nearby, maybe even an endless supply.

"The cavern," she whispered. Turning a notebook page, she drew a picture of the cavern from the side showing the control platform near the top of the page and the water pool near the bottom. Adding a line from the floor to the platform, she drew arrows showing the direction of the water going up the winding ramp to the platform then out the pipe back to the water pool.

"It works!" she thought. "The pool is an endless supply of water!" Excited about her solution, she wondered how long of a water hose she would need as she filled in details of her drawing: levers on the platform, stars in the sky, floor vents, a stick person—herself working the controls—and finally giant droplets complete with trailing lines to show them falling...

She stopped.

The droplets were falling.

"Gravity."

She studied the arrows traveling up from the pool. How would she get water up the path?

A pump—she needed some kind of pump.

No worries, they had a pump on the farm. Jake added one to the picture and another thought struck her. The pump would not run forever, it would stop once it ran out of gas. How long would that be? Longer than seven minutes for sure.

But how would she get the pump to the cavern? Another problem. The pump weighed a ton! It was not too heavy to move a little here or there, but the cavern was just too far away. Perhaps a wheelbarrow would help, but the mushy field would be difficult, and how would she get it across the stream...

The stream. There is plenty of water in the stream.

Jake turned to another page. This time, however, her picture of the cavern was much smaller and placed at the bottom right portion of the page. She added the tree, the forest, and the stream.

"Yes!" she exclaimed. "The stream is much higher than even the cavern's platform. The water can flow down from the stream, no pump is necessary, and it would run forever!"

Turning her attention back to the diary, Jake checked the paper towels. She tossed the soaked ones and replaced them. Satisfied with her work Jake ran outside to what her dad simply called "the garage." The place was huge and it contained a number of tools, parts, and other items needed to maintain or repair just about everything they had on the farm. The previous owners had loved cars, and they built this elaborate heated building complete with underground maintenance pits.

Mid-stride, Jake clicked one of the many garage door remotes. She had taken it from the little basket by the back door when she exited. She reached the garage just as one of the four doors had risen high enough so that she could enter without ducking her head. On the back wall, suspended from pegs, were hoses of every size.

"Well," she said, retrieving a ladder. "Better get started!"

Chapter 12

EVERYTHING BUT THE "OINK"

Aaron placed the last of the backpack's contents on the floor. Arranging the items by size in rows and columns, he confirmed once more that the diary was missing. Feeling inside the pack's various pockets, he uncovered mashed food particles. The light-purple sticky stain on his fingers smelled like grape drink.

Gross, I should have cleaned this out long ago.

His stomach growled. He had not eaten for a while and he missed his mom's homemade breakfasts. His sleep had been restful and long—according to his watch he had already been here for more than ten hours.

I hope the Amish boy found the diary.

As if on cue, he heard footsteps from the cavern's passageway.

"Good morning," the Amish boy called. He carried a bag and a towel-wrapped package.

"Hey," Aaron returned the greeting. "Is that the diary? Did you find it?" But even as he asked, the smell coming from the towel told him otherwise.

"No, it is nowhere in the tree passageways." He placed the wrapped object on the ground next to Aaron. "I also looked around the tree. I retraced our steps from where I first found you but found nothing."

Aaron stared into the distance, frustrated.

"I'm sorry Aaron. I don't think it is here. I'm certain that if you had it when you came through the portal, I would've seen it."

Was it possible? Had it fallen out before he came back in time? He had hoped that he lost it after coming through the portal, or when he had been dragged to the tree. Jake might have been right. Maybe he should have listened to her—

"Oh, no!"

"What?" the Amish boy asked.

Aaron shook his head and ran his hands through his hair. "That's got to be it."

"What are you talking about?"

"Jake. I just remembered that before I jumped into the vortex, Jake was running and yelling at me." Aaron massaged his temples.

"I'm afraid I don't understand."

"She must have seen the diary fall out as I was jumping into the vortex."

Silence.

"What will we do?" the Amish boy asked.

Aaron shook his head. "I'm not sure. Maybe the diary has the answers, but maybe it didn't. I guess we'll just have to figure this out on our own."

"I'll help you. Let me know what you need. But you might be here for some time. I think we need to go into town and have your leg examined."

"I suppose you are right," Aaron said, not wanting to think about how long he might be trapped here. "By the way, what's in the towel?"

"Oh, right." The boy brightened. "I almost forgot—I brought

you some breakfast." The boy unwrapped the towel, and a strange but appealing smell of meat and maple syrup filled the space. Aaron's stomach responded by growling once more.

"Smells great," Aaron said. "But it looks a little funny. What is it?"

"Here." The boy handed him a plate and fork. "What is it? You don't know?"

"Meatloaf?" Aaron replied, uncertain.

The Amish boy scrunched his face. "I don't know what meatloaf is, but surely you have had Scrapple."

Aaron raised his eyebrows. "Scrapple?"

"It is my favorite breakfast meal. Try it."

Aaron shrugged and took a small forkful—meat and syrup, the combination was strange. "Here goes!" he said, taking a bite. The syrup blended with a taste that was kind of like ham or maybe sausage, then corn. His mouth watered. Whatever it was, it was good. "Not bad. Different. But good." He took a bigger bite. "Why is it called Scrapple?"

"Because," the boy answered, "it's made from the left-over pig scraps."

Aaron stopped chewing. "Say again?"

"Well it is made from pig scraps that are too small to be used for anything else."

The mental pictures Aaron formed were not pleasant.

The boy continued, not noticing his friend's discomfort, "You boil the scraps, take out the bones, add some flour and cornmeal, then form it into a loaf." The boy beamed.

"Mom says it is everything from the pig but the oink!" He laughed aloud.

"Hmm," Aaron said. *Maybe this is why Mom never told me how they make hot dogs.*

Everything but the "Oink"

"Once it is formed into a loaf, you cut a piece off and fry it in a pan. Covering it with syrup is my favorite way to eat it. That is why I made it that way for you. Sometimes I have it with eggs too!"

Aaron nodded. The boy was proud. Truth was, it did taste good. "Thanks again," he said, scraping the fork along the plate to get the last of the syrup. "That hit the spot."

"Good! I have something else for you." The boy took out a large cloth bag filled with Amish clothes.

"What are these for?"

"We need to get you to Dr. Adler," the boy explained. "But you cannot go in your present clothes. No one here wears those kinds of shoes or pants. You need to look like you belong here."

Why hadn't I thought of that? I need to add that to the diary to remember later—if I ever see it again.

"I brought some of my clothes for you to use," the boy said. "You are a little bigger than I am, but they should work."

The boy helped Aaron remove his socks, shoes, and the splint to help him change. He depended on the boy for everything—food, being able to move around, even changing his clothes. It was a bit disconcerting.

Taking the Amish shirt, he struggled to figure out how to close it—there were no buttons. It took a moment before he realized that the hooks on one side of the shirt were supposed to loop through the eyes on the other. Next came the pants. The suspenders were actually kind of cool.

"No belts, eh?" he asked.

"No," the boy replied. "Just suspenders." He noticed Aaron looking at his waist. "Anything the matter?"

"Yeah, what's the story with the zipper?"

"What do you mean?"

"Well the pants don't have a zipper. How do I, you know, close everything up?"

The boy laughed. "Pull the flap over and connect the hook on the right."

Aaron laughed. "Argh, it's like I'm some type of pirate or something!" The clothes were itchy against his skin. *Must be because the fabric is a lot coarser than what I'm used to.*

Dark socks, heavy thick brown boots, and a straw-brimmed hat completed the outfit.

"Good," the Amish boy pronounced. "Although…" the boy pointed at the pant legs, which were a few inches too high. "They are a little short, but they'll have to do."

"Before we go, let's put everything back inside my backpack. I want to take my stuff with me."

"What is that gray patch?" the boy asked, eyeing the bottom of the pack.

Aaron smiled. "Oh, that is duct tape! I used it to fix the hole. It should hold for a while until I get a new one. I'm not taking any more chances. Nothing is going to fall out now."

To save time, Aaron let the boy put everything back into the pack. "I have a question," the boy asked. "Why did you line everything in rows?"

"I wanted to take an inventory to make sure nothing else was missing," Aaron responded.

"And?"

"I think I have everything, with one exception."

The boy slung the backpack over his shoulder. "What?"

"A flashlight."

"A what?"

Too early, Aaron thought. He remembered reading that flashlights had been invented around 1900 but they might not have been very popular by this time. Maybe not everyone has heard of them yet. "A flashlight is a lamp that you can turn on and off. It doesn't use kerosene, instead it uses batteries. I heard the early ones could only be turned on briefly, in flashes, which is how they got their name."

Aaron half hopped half walked while leaning on the boy as they made their way out of the cavern. "Anyway," Aaron added between grimaces. "I hope the flashlight fell out with the diary before I got here. If someone in this time finds it, it would create quite a stir."

Chapter 13

THE MAGIC LANTERN

Sitting on a large rock some distance from his house, Samuel examined the object. The sun reflected off its slick, shiny surface. Having never seen anything like it, Samuel inspected the strange canister. It was medium sized, about seven inches long. He tapped the small round glass circle on one end. About one-third down from the glass, he pressed a red button. Light shot out from the glass. Shocked, Samuel dropped the object.

After a moment, he picked it up and shook it. He heard movement inside. Twisting the top, Samuel separated the glass from the rest of the object, and the light went out as the lid popped off. Inside lay two small cylinders. Tipping the object, one of the smaller pieces fell out.

This smaller object was more solid. Nothing rattled when Samuel shook it. One end was flat, and the other had a small nipple protruding from the middle. The second smaller tube was identical. Both were adorned with letters and a picture of a lightning bolt.

Lightning in a tube? he wondered.

He replaced the smaller pieces back inside the canister, sealed the lid, and pushed the red button once more. This time nothing happened.

No light. Samuel shook the device, pressing the button repeatedly. Nothing.

A magic lantern? he considered. *This must have something to do with Sarah's story. She and that boy are hiding something—probably about that tree. I've got to go back.*

⁇

Samuel gazed into the large, gaping, inverted "V" of intertwined trunks. He had seen twin trees before. The young samplings, which were too close at birth, bonded together over time. Their existence became dependent on each other. If anything happened to one—rot, insect infestation, disease—it would affect the other. They were truly connected in life and would follow each other in death.

Samuel shuddered. His brother, *his twin,* had died just after they had been born. He had learned this after overhearing a conversation between his parents the night of his tenth birthday. Samuel awoke from hearing his mother crying. Creeping quietly through the house, he heard his father comforting her.

"Elizabeth, do not torture yourself. God has a plan and that was for one of our boys to live and the other to join him in heaven," his father had said.

"I keep seeing his small body…so frail and tiny," his mother replied between sobs. "Samuel was such a large child. The more he thrived, the sicker little Daniel got."

From that moment on Samuel believed he had somehow robbed his brother of life. Although he never asked, he wondered if his parents felt the same way.

Looking at the twin trees—brothers—fused together, it occurred to Samuel that the haunting emptiness he sometimes felt was due to the loss of his *other half* so early in life.

Clearing his head, he circled the tree looking for anything that would help him to understand what Sarah and the boy might be hiding. The ground, the tree, the crevices, nothing seemed unusual with any of them. Perhaps the answer was inside.

Getting on all fours, he poked his head in. The fit was tight but not too bad. Crawling forward, blackness enveloped him. Samuel paused, waiting for his eyes to adjust. Muted images appeared gray and washed out.

Now would be a good time to have a working lightning tube.

Taking the metallic object, he pressed the side button once more. Again, no light emitted. Frustrated, he threw the tube outside and searched with his hands inside the tree. Damp, mossy, and cool, he found that one corner held a small pile of sticks—the likely home of some forest creature. Behind the nest, he spied an area where the twin trees overlapped. Was there a hidden compartment? Samuel stretched forward to investigate when he heard a twig snap.

He froze. Was that talking he heard?

Something—or someone—is outside.

Samuel struggled and caught his pants on the tree as he backed out, hurrying to find whatever or whoever was traipsing through the forest. He gave a strong yank and the material tore, freeing him. Now the sound of voices was unmistakable.

Who is that?

"You are doing good." He heard one voice say. "Just continue to lean on me."

It was Sarah's friend!

About sixty feet away, from behind a group of wild bushes, the boy emerged, but he was not alone. There was another boy, taller and wearing ill fitting clothes. He limped alongside the first boy, using him for support. They made slow progress. Where had they come from and what were they doing there? And how did the one boy get injured?

Determined to find where they had come from, Samuel waited for them to pass, then went in the opposite direction. He examined the forest—grass had been bent from their footsteps. There were broken bush branches and the natural position of various plants had been disturbed. Following these, he traced back their path—until the signs vanished.

Where had they come from?

It was as if they had simply appeared in the middle of the forest and walked out. He scanned the area once more, but no trails led off in any direction, other than the one he had come from. The only unusual part of the forest he could find was the enormous ancient-looking tree that towered in front of him.

Another strange tree, he thought. His skin tingled, forming goosebumps. He had that feeling of being watched and glanced over his shoulder, fearing the boys had returned. Then he laughed. There was no possible way they could have gotten back there, especially with the boy's injured leg. He would have heard them for sure.

He paused, taking in the silence.

That was it—the silence. The lack of noise surrounded him. He felt as if a large predator waited nearby, sending the forest creatures into hiding. It was time to leave. He committed this place to memory so that he could investigate later. Before leaving, he got his bearings so he could retrieve the lightning tube that he had left behind.

When Samuel reached the twin trees, the magic lantern was gone. He searched and searched, but it was nowhere to be found.

Chapter 14

UPHILL BATTLE

Sitting alongside the creek, Jake cupped her hands and splashed water to cool her face. Carrying the hoses had been more of a chore than she had expected and although it was late fall, the Indian summer made the work even more challenging.

This was Jake's favorite time of year. The field's crops were in, sweatshirts were unpacked, and the winter's bite was not yet in the air. These were the precious few days before everything went dormant. Life went quiet and still until the buds of spring. The air was crisp but not harsh, and the nights were just cold enough to snuggle under thick bed covers.

Jake should have been happy. The Amish boy's diary was supposed to be a gift that documented their incredible journeys. How had everything gone so wrong? It was not supposed to be this hard. Anxiety made her rub her stomach where the nervous knot was growing.

What if can't get into cavern? What if he can't come back?

But that was not possible. She had seen both of their handwriting in the diary—that meant they would be together again. It had to turn out okay. Or did it? Her mind stopped short. A thread of a thought developed. The diary could include both of their handwriting, but that did not necessarily mean Aaron would return to the present.

Why hadn't she thought of it before? It was so obvious.

If both she and Aaron went back in time, they could have filled in the diary with information from the past and left it for their future selves. Maybe it was not the Amish boy that left the diary for them—maybe she and Aaron left it for themselves because they could not return to the present. Maybe the diary contained a warning!

She stared into the distance, lost in thought, wondering if it could be true.

It can't be! She concluded. The Amish boy's note that accompanied the diary said nothing about that. No! There must be another answer.

Jake stood, brushed off her pants, and picked up the hoses, pushing her fears aside. She would finish what she started. Her mother was right—an idle mind is the devil's workshop. She needed to stay busy, solve the problem, and forget about what had gone wrong.

Jake half dragged, half carried, the longest hose to the tree's entrance. She would use this hose to snake down the passageway, through the helium room, into the tunnel, and onto the platform. The next hose she connected to the first, repeating this process over and over again until she reached the stream. Plunging her hands into the water, she cleaned off the dirt and grime. She found a nice deep spot to place one end of the hose.

She gathered a foot or two of the hose and created some slack to ensure that a small tug would not pull it out of the stream. Jake nodded with pride. *Pretty smart!* she thought. How many times had she pulled the power cord out of an outlet when vacuuming because she did not have enough slack? Too often! She couldn't afford a similar problem with this project.

Unfortunately, the water's current moved the hose, pushing it downstream and the end floated to the top. Her hands went to her hips, and she scrunched her forehead while tapping her foot. She needed a heavy object to hold the hose in place.

A rock! That was it. Jake searched the banks of the creek—lots of small pebbles, some sticks, but no big rocks.

Are you kidding me? She thought. *I can't find a dumb rock!*

Crossing the stream, she continued her search in the fields. The plow frequently uncovered large rocks, and soon she found a perfect-sized one. Jake rolled the rock end over end to the water's edge. She continued until it covered the repositioned hose. It was heavy enough to keep the hose from moving, but she positioned it over the metal portion of the hose so it would not crush the tube and stop the flow of water.

She tugged the hose this way and that.

That should hold you! She concluded.

Jake ran to the tree, grabbed the other end of the hose, and checked for running water—so far nothing.

Maybe I beat the water here.

She dropped the hose on the ground and waited.

Nothing.

Frustrated, she stared into the hose, angling it so that the sunlight shone into the tube.

Still nothing.

Jake flipped back her braided pony tails and tucked a couple of loose strands behind her ear. Tilting her head, she held the hose to her ear—no gurgling sound. The setup was not working. For some reason the water was not flowing.

She threw the hose's end down in frustration and marched back following its length. Coming to the first place where the hoses joined, she quickly unscrewed them to see if the water had made it that far.

Again, nothing!

It did not make sense. She stomped to the next section and disconnected it as well.

Same result.

Each time, she found the same thing. Even the hose closest to the stream was empty.

Maybe the hose popped out of the water.

When she came over the small bank, she saw it was still held in place.

Then she realized the problem was the stream's bank. She had not accounted for it when making her plans. Opening her backpack, Jake pulled out the drawing, adjusting it by the small bank and realized the problem. The first section of hose went from under the water *up* the side of the bank then back down into the forest. The water first needed to go up, then back down.

She sighed realizing the answer to the problem.

About a year ago, her dad taught her how to use a siphon. They had run out of gas for their chainsaw, and her father had decided to take some fuel from their car's tank rather than running into town.

"You see Jake," her dad had said while placing a red container on the ground next to the car. "We need to get the gas from the tank up here in the car down into this container."

Jake watched while he brought out a long clear tube and fed it into the car's gas tank.

"I've got one end in the car here, but if I put the other end lower toward the canister, nothing happens." He knelt and held the tube toward the ground. "See, no gas, even though the tank is higher than the canister. The gas has to first come up and out of the tank, then back down."

"How do you make it do that?" she asked.

"You know the answer to that! You do it all the time."

Jake stared at him confused. She never did this!

He continued, "How do you drink soda from a fast food restaurant?"

"Through a straw?" she said, but had not made the connection.

Her dad nodded. "Yeah, you *suck* the liquid up."

"You're saying you have to suck the gas out through the hose? Yuk!"

"Well that's why I use a clear hose. That way I can see the gas. I need to get it a little higher than the gas cap, then it can flow down into to the canister."

Jake sort of got it.

"Watch," her dad had said. He pulled the tube to his mouth and inhaled. The gas rose, creeping toward his mouth. Jake noticed her dad kept a close eye on how high the gas went, and when it got to within about a foot of his mouth, he stopped and quickly moved the hose into the canister.

It had worked!

Jake lifted her eyebrows in surprise. "Neat, but why does it keep going?"

"Well a liquid always finds its level," he said.

That didn't help, she thought and her expression must have said the same thing.

Her dad laughed. "What I mean is that the tank is up here." He pointed at the car. "As long as the tube is below the tank, the gas will flow. Once the tube goes higher than the tank, it will stop."

Jake shook her head slowly.

"Look," he said and lifted the canister so that it made a U-shape with the tube. As soon as one end of the U was above the tank, the gas stopped flowing. The bottom of the tube was filled with gas, but it could not get up and into the canister from that height. Her dad moved the tube up and down but the place where the gas stopped did not change—it always matched the level of the gas in the tank.

"Weird," Jake said.

"Cool," her dad replied with a wink. "While it is below the tank, it will keep flowing until it's gone. The key is getting the gas up and over. It is literally downhill from there!" He lowered the canister and the gas began to flow again.

That was what she needed to do now. She had to get the water over the bank of the stream. Then it would work. After a few frustrating attempts, and having nearly turned blue in the face from the exertion, it finally worked. Water flowed from the first section and puddled on the ground. She connected the next hose and soon water flowed out the other side.

Woohoo! she cheered. An endless supply of water! She could keep the cavern open forever.

Don't worry Aaron, she thought as she connected the remaining hoses. *I'm coming!*

Chapter 15
THE APOTHECARY

Jostling around in the back of the carriage, Aaron grunted with each bump. He had thought that getting in would prove to be a challenge, but the Amish boy had somehow maneuvered him up and in. Aaron was not sure why the boy could take the horse and buggy—he certainly would not have been able to drive his dad's truck if they were back in his time, but things were different here.

Traveling along the pitted dirt road, Aaron watched as the barn grew smaller and smaller in the distance. He imagined the scene as the boy described the barn's raising.

"Honestly, it was one of my favorite memories. The day started early, well earlier than normal. I could hear my mother and father moving about the house but I knew they wanted me to stay in bed. I hadn't slept much because of my excitement, and finally I could wait no longer. My mother had already made a large, hearty breakfast of eggs, meat, and thick syrup. It was wonderful. Even before the sun rose, I heard horse footfalls as carriage after carriage brought families from around the community.

"We had a lot to prepare before the big day. A few families who lived close by had come over the last few days before the raising to help clear the land and prepare the lumber and such. But today everyone was coming. A barn raising is quite an event for us. Everyone is expected to help. Entire families arrived and all my friends were there. One man was our expert carpenter. He was the leader, and most of the elders were in charge of different activities.

"Me and some other boys my age helped carry and cut wood. Ever since then whenever I get a blister, it reminds me of that day, and I get a warm feeling inside.

"Sarah was there too, of course, but the girls had different work. They had helped the mothers prepare the food that kept everyone fed throughout the day.

"Sometimes when there wasn't much we could do to help, we would play games in the yard. The time passed by quickly and I grew very tired. By the time the shadows started getting long, the sides and the roof were up. I could not believe it. Once it got too dark to see, the work stopped so that no one would get hurt. After that, it only took a couple more days to finish."

Aaron thought about how they could build such a large structure in such a short period of time. He laughed when he thought it was the Amish equivalent of *Extreme Home Makeover*. He imagined an Amish elder getting the rest of the community to yell, "Buggy driver—move that buggy!"

The dust from the dirt road flew up and settled on his seat. Riding in the back of the pickup truck back home was very similar. The farmland had not changed much in one hundred years. He remembered asking his dad if they could get a buggy and got that *you've-got-to-be-kidding-me* look in return. Yet, here he was, riding in one now, wearing Amish clothes one hundred years in the past.

The Amish boy turned the buggy on to another dirt road, and

The Inverted Cavern

Aaron saw the town—his town. But it did not look anything like the one in his day. There were no paved roads or parking meters. Where the surplus shop was in his time, there was now some type of wooden butcher shop shack. There were a few masonry and brick buildings here and there. Nearly everyone walked from place to place, only a few bicycles and even fewer carriages dotted the road.

One carriage that was going in the opposite direction was led by a horse that went to the bathroom right in the middle of the street! The carriage continued as if nothing unusual happened. The pile steamed. *Gross,* Aaron thought, then he noticed the rest of the street was littered with similar piles. People walked by adjusting their paths and strides to miss the mounds. *Thank goodness it's not too hot today or this place would reek!* he thought. *How could these people possibly live this way?*

A moment later a young man with a shovel ran out into the street and scooped a pile. He ran to a side road where an open trailer was hitched to a rather large horse. There, he deposited the manure on top of a growing pile.

Noticing Aaron's disturbed look, the Amish boy commented, "It makes great fertilizer for the fields."

"I'm sure," Aaron replied, unimpressed.

"The family who removes the town's waste earns considerable money selling it to farms in the area."

Aaron shook his head in disgust. What a job. That boy who rushed out for another shovelful was around his age. He could only imagine his dad getting him out of bed each day to go scoop the poop. Bizarre.

As they made their way through the small town, Aaron noticed a large impressive building ahead and to the left. He immediately recognized it: *Soda Jerks.* Only now, it was new and definitely not an ice cream shop.

The Amish boy drove the carriage another block before stopping in the front of what had to be the largest house in town. The structure had a massive front porch that wrapped around one side. Flowers and bushes adorned the front lawn and trimmed the walkway. A large porch swing hung to the left of an ornately covered wooden door with inlaid stain glass.

"What's this about?" Aaron asked.

"We are going to the doctor, of course."

"Here?" Aaron asked. "This is someone's house."

"Of course it is. This is where Dr. Adler lives."

"But why aren't we going to his office? Why would we come here?"

"Aaron, this is his office *and* his house. I don't understand what you are asking. In your time do you not go to doctors' houses?"

Aaron laughed aloud. He imagined that the doctors in his time lived on massive estates in gated communities. He guessed they would not even let folks come into the subdivision much less near their houses.

"No, not quite," he responded. "We go to a clinic, or a hospital."

The Amish boy tilted his head.

"Never mind," Aaron said. "Frankly I don't like going to a clinic anyway. They smell funny."

Aaron turned the front door knob and tried to push it open. "Here, I'll help," the Amish boy said. Then someone pulled from inside.

"Here boys, let me help you," an elderly man said with a thick foreign accent. "I saw you come up the walk and I thought I'd give you a hand. This door is heavy, most folks have a hard time opening it."

He helped Aaron over the threshold, which was decorated with a number of small pearl-colored tiles. Beautiful richly dark woodwork paneled the interior. A grand staircase rose from his right, a chandelier lighting the way. To the left, a credenza covered with white doilies and various expensive-looking knick knacks flanked the hallway. A black bowler hat sat atop a carved coatrack.

THE INVERTED CAVERN

The man directed them in. "Please have a seat in the waiting room. I am just finishing up with another patient." He left through a cloth covered door, while they moved to a small sitting room. The inside was filled with expensive looking furniture, side tables, and lamps that reminded Aaron of stained-glass windows. Wood burned in the fireplace. The room had no other visitors.

"This is amazing," Aaron said. "I know doctors make a lot of money but even in this small town?"

"Oh no," the Amish boy replied. "From what I understand, Dr. Adler comes from a very wealthy German family. He's some type of nobility from what I've heard."

That explains the accent, Aaron thought.

The door to the examining room opened, and a man dressed in a three-piece suit came out and took the hat off the rack.

"Thank you again, Dr. Adler," he said, shaking the doctor's hand. Taking hold of the door he too struggled to open it, and Aaron stifled a snicker.

"Okay boys, come on in please," Dr. Adler said.

The doctor's office reminded Aaron of visiting a museum. The room was about the same size of the sitting room. A large glass cabinet lined the wall closest to the door. It contained an assortment of bottles with various hand scripted labels. Some bottles were clear and held strange colored tonics. Others were quite small and intriguing. On top of the cabinet was a human skull. Seeing this, Aaron eyed the Amish boy, who sat stoically. On the opposite wall were shelves overflowing with leather-bound books. A small desk stood nearby, and the doctor sat in its accompanying chair. To the side of the desk was an odd-shaped object on the floor—round and bulbous at the bottom, the object narrowed to a small neck near the top, then flared out. Aaron leaned forward peering inside and saw a disgusting brown chunky liquid. *Yuk,* he thought *a tobacco spittoon.*

"Have a seat," the doctor said, motioning toward the small, tan examination table. "It's not often that your kind come to see me."

As they had discussed before arriving, the Amish boy would do most of the talking. He had been worried that Aaron's accent and strange vocabulary would raise questions that they would prefer not to answer.

"I believe my friend has broken his leg. I have splinted it, but he needs medicine to manage the pain." He motioned to Aaron who simply nodded.

The doctor brought his chair closer and rolled up Aaron's pant leg. Aaron held back a yelp. He was certain he would faint as tears welled in his eyes while the doctor examined him.

"Sorry, son, I know it hurts, but I am afraid in a moment it may hurt more. The bone has not been set properly. I've got to correct it, or it will not heal." Dr. Adler opened a door to the glass cabinet and removed a couple bottles that Aaron had seen earlier.

"Because the correction is substantial, I'll give you an anesthetic to make you sleep. If it was minor, I could set the bone while you bite on a bit of leather."

The doctor took out a large basin and stood. "I shall return in a moment." He left and closed the door behind him.

The Amish boy asked, "Are you okay?"

"Well I guess so. At first I thought he was going to have to put the bone in place with me awake. I don't think I could do that. But in many ways, coming here is better than going to a clinic in my time. It's much more comforting to be in a home, even if it's one with skulls on a cabinet."

"Don't worry, Aaron. I will make sure no harm comes to you."

"Thanks," Aaron replied, though there was nothing the boy could do to stop him from worrying.

Dr. Adler returned, carrying the large basin, which he set on top of the desk while pushing books and papers to the side. Waves rippled through the clear liquid. For a moment, it reminded Aaron of the time cavern.

"I'm going to use these bandages to set your cast," the doctor said, interrupting Aaron's thoughts. He placed the bandages next to the basin and then took a large canister from the shelf of tonics. He set it next to the bandages along with a long glass rod. Finally the doctor removed a dark-green glass bottle, and pulled out the stopper. Holding a folded handkerchief tightly over the top, he tipped the bottle and doused the material.

"All right," he said. "I'm going to begin by placing this over your nose and mouth. It will smell a little strange, but I need you to breathe deeply. Soon you will fall asleep. Okay?"

Aaron glanced over at the Amish boy who, for the first time, appeared a bit concerned but nodded his approval.

"Okay," Aaron replied. "I'm ready."

Groggily, Aaron opened his eyes. He found it difficult to focus at first—his vision blurry. Then he felt the pain shooting through his leg. Shaking his head to clear his thoughts, he studied the room in which he lay on the examination table.

"Take this to the apothecary," he heard the doctor say while handing the Amish boy a small piece of paper. "He will be able to fill the prescription." His friend took the paper and folded it in half.

"He is waking, Doctor." The Amish boy pointed.

"Good, good," the doctor said, helping Aaron to move his legs over the side of the table and sit up. "Yes, all is good. Your friend here will take you to get your pain medication." The doctor left the room and returned with a Y-shaped crutch. "Here, this will help you get around."

Still a bit disoriented, Aaron simply nodded to the doctor. After a few moments, he and the Amish boy ambled their way out of the office to the carriage. Maneuvering his leg was even more challenging now, thanks to the thick, heavy cast.

"Stay here. I will go and get the medicine," the Amish boy said. The apothecary is just down this street.

"No, wait! I want to go."

"Why?"

"Are you kidding? I've got to see the place. In my time, that building is an ice cream parlor."

As they approached the building, Aaron noticed that the red-and-white striped awnings and the *Soda Jerks* sign were gone, although the rest looked unchanged.

"Whoa, look out," the boy shouted as he stopped Aaron from placing the crutch in a rather large pile of horse manure.

"I guess I should spend more time looking down!"

Inside the apothecary, the tiled floors were different and the tables and booths were gone. Instead, shelves lined the walls holding numerous items for sale. Framed advertisements flanked the sides of the shelves. They consisted of just words typeset in different sized letters in one or two colors. One caught his eye:

Wild Cherry
TONIC
For the cure of
All Nervous Disorders

THE INVERTED CAVERN

Dyspepsia
Jaundice
Bilious Complaints
Loss of Appetite and General Debility
SOLD HERE

Aaron liked the "Wild Cherry" part but had no idea what a "Bilious Complaint" was. He wondered where the disclaimers were. Television commercials always ended with disclaimers: "could cause redeye, seizure, heart attack, depression..." and on and on. Who would take that stuff?

He and the Amish boy approached the ornate bar, which in this time was an ordering counter. The mirror behind the counter was still there, but it was hidden by glass shelves holding a large assortment of rubber-stoppered containers, like those in the doctor's office. Underneath these shelves, numerous small cubby-type drawers, like those found in a roll-top desk were hand labeled. There were hundreds of them.

"I don't understand," Aaron said. "The doctor had a lot of jars and tonics in his office. Why do we have to come here?"

"Not so loud," the boy cautioned, not wanting to draw too much attention. "He told me there are still some items that need a prescription and he didn't have the ingredients to make what you need to control the pain."

They stepped up to the counter, and the Amish boy unfolded and handed the paper to the man.

Pulling out a large ledger, which was similar to the ones Aaron had seen in old hotels, the man wrote the date and the details from the paper the Amish boy had handed him. Aaron noticed a large R and small x at the top of the page. What the heck did Rx mean? He had seen it in his time as well.

He decided to ask, trying to sound as formal as possible. "Excuse me, sir, I'm curious. Would you be able to tell me what the Rx means on that piece of paper?"

The man scowled, and Aaron wondered if he had crossed some unknown social line. But the man's face lightened. "You know, no one has ever asked me that before, young man. You are the first. I would be happy to tell you." He held the piece of paper toward the boys. "You see, this writing from Dr. Adler tells me how to make your medicine. These are instructions for what type of ingredients to add and how much of each."

"It's a recipe," Aaron interrupted.

"Exactly," the man said. "Rx is an abbreviation for the Latin word that means recipe—specifically, 'take thou.'"

"Cool!" Aaron said, but quickly stifled his enthusiasm. Given the look of curiosity on the man's face as well as the Amish boy's disapproving frown, he figured 'cool' was not a word commonly used in the late nineteenth century. The man behind the counter went about his work, taking different items and placing them in a clay bowl. He pounded and ground the items into a powder.

"Before you ask," he said without glancing up. "It's called a mortar and pestle. I use it to make the medicine. You are quite lucky you know. Dr. Adler travels extensively, and this recipe is from a colleague in Germany—a Dr. Hoffman. That doctor works for a company with a funny name." The pharmacist paused from his work, trying to remember. "It was named after an animal—bear—I believe."

Aaron stifled a laugh as he knew the real answer. The company was Bayer not Bear.

His prescription must be for Bayer aspirin.

Chapter 16
THE OPAQUE DOORWAY

Jake fed the end of the hose into the receiving tube on the platform in the cavern. Water flowed freely. She took a moment to stare at the setup, admiring her ingenuity.

Aaron isn't the only one who can figure stuff out!

Turning to the main control lever, she pulled it forward. The vent's noise rose and suddenly the hose yanked out and whizzed by. Instinctively her hands covered her head and she ducked just in time. Was she hit? Her hair was wet. Was she bleeding? Inspecting her hands, she saw only water.

What happened?

She found the answer out of the corner of her eye. The hose hung from the wall at eye level. She had forgotten that turning on the cavern also closed the entrance. The hose must have been pulled free when the tunnel collapsed.

Jake studied where the hose met the wall. It appeared cemented in place, but water continued to trickle out of it like some kind of fountain sculpture. Whatever held it there was not tight enough to pinch off the flow.

She imagined the hose suspended four feet high throughout the length of the tunnel, exiting through the middle of the atom symbol in the helium room. But that assumed there were separate doorways at each end and the tunnel was hollow between them. Maybe the entire tunnel was solid when shut. What would happen if someone was in there when it closed? Jake shuddered.

The vents stopped when the water ran out. The platform lever automatically moved back to the "off" position. Immediately, the entrance opened and the hose fell to the floor. Jake rushed through the tunnel, keeping her morbid wall-crushing thoughts at bay. She needed to retrieve as much of the hose as possible. With enough slack, the hose should stay in place.

Feeding the hose once more into the intake tube, she stared at the symbols etched on the pipe: $H2O$. While it seemed like a long time ago that they had discovered the cavern, it had really only been a couple of months. In fact, she had only known Aaron a few days longer than that, and yet she could not remember life before him—now he was gone—perhaps trapped or hurt.

Was he gone for good? *No*, she thought. She would find him and bring him home.

She brushed her fingers over the symbol's engraved image, examining them. *Who made this? And why did they use atomic symbols?* An answer started to form at the edge of her consciousness, but just as quickly as it had arrived, it disappeared again. Confused but undaunted, she approached the main lever. This time, the hose lay snaked across the floor with plenty of slack, her backpack pinned the end near the tube. She pulled the lever, and the hose snapped into position, but the backpack stayed in place.

It worked!

The water flowed, the vents sounded, and the stars appeared.

Everything worked! To be sure, Jake waited a full half hour to confirm that the portal stayed open. While she waited, she passed the time by taking out her notebook and the diary. Even with her valiant attempt to recover the pages, a number of them were ruined. Some of them could be read, usually the ones with strong dark lines and even on those the ink had bled out from the script. On these pages, she could feel the indentation of the words in the paper, as if someone had pressed hard while writing.

Some pages contained only pictures—drawings of lever positions with arrows pointing to cavern ceiling constellations. Details and star names were hard to read. Scanning the pages, she wondered if maybe Aaron had left her a note about what to do. But it was like looking for a needle in a haystack. This diary had suffered years of abuse, had been buried for a century, jostled in a backpack, submerged, and dried out. It was a wonder it had not yet fallen completely apart.

After twenty minutes had passed, she was impressed that the water continued to flow and the portal stayed strong. Even the pounding sounds of the tonal vents no longer bothered her. *I guess I've gotten used to them.*

Leafing through the diary, one page caught her attention. The words were some of the clearest she had seen in the diary. "Future" was written near the top and "Inverted" near the bottom. On that same page and to the right in big capital letters with double underlines was written:

<u>NOT THE MOON SETTING!!</u>

The handwriting was unmistakable—it was hers!

In the middle of the page was a picture of a tree, and below it, a big smiling half circle. Above the tree another half circle, but this one upside down like a frown.

Her thirty minutes had expired. She shut the diary. It was time. She was going back in. Moving aside the spray bottles of helium in her backpack, she made room for the diary. She did not know why she was bringing all this stuff, but she wanted to be prepared for anything.

Before going into the portal, she inspected the cavern ceiling and saw the moon clearly in the targeting crosshairs. She hesitated, remembering the words of warning: "NOT THE MOON SETTING." Brushing her fears aside, she went in.

Standing underneath the canopy of the tree, Jake checked the portal, saying a silent prayer for it to stay open. She set her watch alarm for one hour so she could go back out and double-check the hose and stream—just to make sure everything was all right.

She examined the rings of image screens surrounding her, and intuition told her that walking farther away from the tree would not help to find Aaron. Where else is there?

She studied the tree. Why is it here? It must have a purpose. The other tree contained the cavern itself. A thought struck her. Maybe this one was more than just a tree as well. She carefully inspected the bark. *Can it be that simple? Does this tree have a secret panel?* Finding a similar notch as the tree in the forest, she tried to move it. While it did not slide, it did wiggle a little. Changing tactics, she pushed on it. The notch began to move on its own and slowly sank into the tree. As it receded, a larger section of the tree moved as well. Unlike the forest tree, it was completely silent. After moving inward, the entire section slid into the ground. Blackness remained. Not darkness, but complete blackness.

Jake took a flashlight from her pack and shined it into the abyss.

Nothing. As soon as it the light hit the entrance, it disappeared. *Aaron would not be able to resist this kind of mystery*, she thought. Trepidation rushed over her.

Man, he's probably in there! What is he thinking?!

There was no sign, or note, or anything outside the tree that indicated he had been there. What should she do?

Think it through logically. Step by step.

Jake inched toward the opening and turned her head, concentrating. *Sight doesn't work. Let's try the other senses.* "Hello!" she yelled into the blackness. No echo, no sound. Similar to the light, her voice disappeared into the void. She sniffed but caught no scent.

A feeling of déjà vu came over her as she remembered how she felt when she had entered the forest for the first time. Just like then it seemed as though sound ceased to exist.

Jake checked the portal above once more. She had found herself doing that frequently. Taking out her notebook, she wrote a list of things she knew—or thought she was sure of. Doing that was a trick she had learned from her mother. About a year ago, she had lost an overdue library book, and tore apart her room and most of the house looking for it. Her mother had told her that if she did not find it, she would not only have to pay the late fee, but she would also have to buy the library a new copy.

"Well where was the last place you had it?" her mom had asked.

Jake responded immediately. "I don't know." She could tell by her mom's expression, that she should have thought harder before answering.

"Why don't you write down everything you remember about the last time you read the book. Where were you sitting? What time of day was it? Morning? Afternoon? Were you eating a snack? Take the time to really put yourself back to the moment you last remember having it."

Jake argued, "Why do I have to write it, can't I just tell you?"

Her mom insisted. "Writing things down causes your brain to slow down, and memories you didn't even know were there will come to the surface. Trust me, and don't forget to include everything you can remember—even if it feels 'stupid.'"

Jake tried it. At first she did feel dumb. She wrote: it's a book, its cover is blue, it came from the library…but as she thought, she started to see the book in her mind. She remembered that the last time she had read it, she was near the end of the story. The left side of the book was heavier because the majority of the pages were on that side. The fonts were funny and each chapter started with a picture. Then she remembered the last section she had read and how it made her feel. The book had described an arctic scene that was so realistic that she got a blanket to snuggle under while reading. They always stored their heavy blankets in a shelved closet underneath the stairwell along with their camping equipment.

Suddenly she had remembered. When she was pulling out a blanket, she had set the book on the closet floor. Just then there was a crash upstairs and her mom had yelled. Jake had raced to help.

When she had returned to the storage closet, she opened the door and found the book.

Ever since then Jake was a believer in writing out her thoughts, not only for remembering, but for everything.

She started a list.

- I'm alone in a place without any time (She chuckled after writing this.)
- There is a big tree with an entrance
- I can't see inside

- No light can shine in
- There is no sound

Just because I can't hear or see anything, doesn't mean that nothing is there. There's only one way to know for sure!

Dumping the contents of her pack, Jake unhooked one of the shoulder straps and loosened the clasp to make it as long as possible. Twisting the end of the strap around her hand, she sat on the ground and tossed the pack to the side to see how far it stretched. She guessed about two or three feet. Pulling it back, she practiced a few more times. Each time she got it about the same distance.

Turning to the entrance, she crept forward to the tree. Sitting out front, she knew the pack would reach past the barrier if she tossed it. Loosening her grip on the strap, she prepared to let go if anything tried to pull her inside.

One…

Two…

Three…

In it went, hitting the barrier and vanishing. Instinct took over, and Jake dropped the strap and squeezed her eyes shut. After a moment, she slowly opened them. There was no pack, but the strap lay at her side reaching forward into the blackness where it simply stopped, as if it were cut clean from the rest of the pack. Cautiously, she placed a finger in the strap's loop, yanked quickly, and let go. More of the strap came out of the blackness like a rabbit from a magician's hat. Emboldened, she grabbed and pulled on the strap. She felt the weight of the pack without seeing it.

It's still there, she thought. *I just can't see it.*

As she continued to pull, the backpack slowly emerged from the entrance. Once freed, Jake examined it and found it was fine.

The Opaque Doorway

Twisting the strap around her hand—this time more tightly—Jake stood and twirled the pack in a big circle like some type of martial artist. Repositioning, she moved her arm so that the pack would swing into and out of the entrance. *Weird.* It appeared and disappeared as it swung back and forth.

Jake determined it was safe. After repacking everything, she shouldered the backpack and stared into the tree. Raising her left arm, she reached out quickly poking a finger at the blackness.

Nothing.

She was unharmed.

There was no weird sensation, or anything out of the ordinary. Braver, she thrust her whole arm in, held it there for a count of three, and then brought it back out.

Same result.

Okay, she thought, *this is it.* She held her breath and stepped into the opaque doorway.

Chapter 17
THE SLATE AND HORN BOOK

After taking the medicine, Aaron's pain subsided even though he bounced in the carriage. Given the late hour and the fact that the sun set early this time of year, they decided to wait until morning to return to the tree. But where should they go in the meantime? Aaron could not go home with the Amish boy, and they considered having him stay in the barn, but in the end decided both were too risky. On most days his father woke up early to work in the fields, and he would go to the barn first.

The hayloft might have been a possibility, but with Aaron's broken leg the only way up would have been to use the pulley. No matter how enthusiastically the Amish boy said he could do it, Aaron pushed back. It was too high, too scary, and too risky. There was too much chance of them being seen.

In the end, Aaron's curiosity had solved the problem. Amazed by how different the town had been from his own time, Aaron asked the Amish boy to show him around the area. Instead of going straight home, the boys took the carriage out of town in the opposite direction from where they had come.

What Aaron thought would be an adventure, actually turned out to be quite boring. As it turned out, farms did not look that much different one hundred years in the past. The land and the houses looked much like they did in Aaron's time, except that here there were fewer farms.

The carriage trudged through a pitted road toward a hill that was shadowed by mature trees. At the top, a tiny cemetery came into view, which did not look familiar. Then again, Aaron had not remembered exploring this part of town even in his own time.

"Can we stop?" Aaron asked excitedly.

"Why?"

"I want to look around."

The Amish boy's expression changed. He seemed to wonder why anyone would want to explore a cemetery. Nonetheless, he stopped the carriage.

Two things struck Aaron immediately. The first was how small it was—about the size of his old suburban backyard in Minneapolis. The second was the groupings of graves. From the headstone dates, he could tell that generations of families had been buried in this small graveyard. Their entire lives were lived only within this town. The world for them was a very small place—grandfathers, fathers, wives, and children lived and died here. Exploring farther, Aaron found a lot of gravesites for children, many of them were infants.

"It's so sad."

"What?" the Amish boy asked.

"All of these children—how did they die? Was there some accident?"

The Amish boy shook his head slightly and furrowed his brow. "No, no accident. Mr. Johnson's wife died giving birth to that boy there." He pointed to one headstone. "The others died from sickness in their first year. It's very common and happens to most families. There are few families that don't lose at least one child. It's a part of life."

A part of life? Aaron could not believe his ears. Medical advances over the last century had made infant deaths rare. He could not think of a single person who had lost a brother or sister as an infant. What a tragedy.

"Okay," Aaron said. "Let's get going."

As he climbed back into the carriage, Aaron noticed a small building in the distance. "What's that?"

The boy grabbed the horse's reigns. "That's the schoolhouse. But I heard the teacher is visiting a relative who is ill.

"So is it empty until she returns?"

"Yes, I suppose so."

"Empty!" Aaron's eyes grew wide. "How far away are we from the forest?"

"We've been circling it while we made our way back to the farm. We are on the opposite side. It is over in that direction," he said, pointing to a tree line not too far from where they were.

"I think I know where I'm staying!"

The old schoolhouse sat wedged between two lonely intersecting roads outside of town. A small front porch with a couple of long benches adorned the otherwise simple clapboard structure.

"Children take off their boots and store them here before going into the school," the Amish boy explained, pointing to the benches as he opened the front door.

"I can't believe it isn't locked," Aaron said as they entered.

"Why would it be locked?"

"So no one breaks in and steals anything."

"Why would anyone break into a school? What would they steal? A desk? Slate? And what would they do with it?"

What indeed, Aaron thought. Why *would* anyone break into a school? It was a good question. Still, everyone locked up everything in his time. Had the world become so untrustworthy?

Beyond the threshold a real one-room schoolhouse greeted them. In the very center of the room, a black cast iron wood stove sat, complete with a giant smoke stack reaching through the roof. In front of the stove, wood was piled. Rows of desks lined either side of the stove, facing the front of the room. Aaron had not seen anything like them. Underneath the writing surface was a place for storing materials. From the front of the desk was a piece that formed the chair for the desk in front of it. Where chair legs would have been in a desk from Aaron's time, here were ornate iron latticed supports. All of the desks sat on an unpainted wooden floor.

Four sets of large single-paned windows lined the side walls. In the front was a small chalkboard and to its side sat the teacher's desk. On the opposite side of the board, a small American flag draped down from its pole. A nearby wooden table held a variety of books.

Passing one of the desks, Aaron noticed a small item inside. He sat, reached in, and pulled out a heavy, flat, black object. Framed in wood, it was about the size of a sheet of paper.

"It's a slate," the Amish boy explained, "for working on math problems and practicing writing."

"There's no paper for taking notes?"

"Taking notes?"

"You know, after school you take your notes home to review and study."

"No, no notes. We repeat lessons over and over, to memorize them during class. Paper is not used in schools. When the slate is filled, it is erased and reused."

No paper? That was hard to imagine. Aaron brought home tons of notebooks, assignment worksheets, and folders full of paper that announced everything from karate classes to dates to join the chess club. Most of it was thrown away immediately. What a waste. The slate thing was pretty cool, it could save a bunch of trees.

Walking to the table near the flag, the Amish boy examined a square, flat, wooden object that had a handle. It was paddle shaped, similar to a handheld mirror. Instead of shinny glass, this had paper mounted to it. On the paper was writing. A see-thru sheet covered the entire paddle.

"We learned about those," the Amish boy said. "Years before slates, this is what students used to learn to read."

Aaron took a closer look. The alphabet was printed in both capital and lowercase letters along with samples of syllable sounds. The lower half of the page contained the entire text of the Lord's Prayer from the Bible.

"It's hard to imagine these were ever used in school," the Amish boy said.

Aaron thought about the irony of the boy's statement. His school was so different than this. It was only a single room, had no paper, electricity, computers, whiteboards, or even running water!

"What is that clear sheet covering it?"

"That protects it from damage," the boy explained. "This is made from a ram's horn. The horn is boiled and scraped to make it clear. That's why it's called a hornbook."

The light within the schoolhouse dimmed, turning an orange hue as the sun sunk low in the sky.

"I better get going," the boy said. "Do not light the stove. Someone might see the smoke and investigate."

"Got it."

"I will see you in the morning," he said, heading to the door and leaving Aaron behind.

Chapter 18
DESTRUCTION

The house's occupants, slept quietly and soundly. Soon dawn would break, and everyone would rise. Chores would begin. Now was the time to act! The barn was the first stop. A powerful tool was needed— something heavy. Aha! A sledgehammer. That would do.

Raised with a heave, it was shouldered for the long trek through the forest.

A three-quarters moon and clear night's sky illuminated the way. Chilled by the autumn's night air, but taxed by the weight of the hammer, a cold clammy sweat quickly formed. Standing some distance from where the two Amish boys had walked through the forest, their steps were retraced.

Following the path backward was challenging in the dim moonlight, but soon the great tree appeared from around the bend. The tree was the key! If it were destroyed, the trouble would stop and everything would return to normal. But how? If the entrance could be closed...

The tree was a sight to behold; the moonlit shadows from the bark created rich earthy textures. Searching the crevasses, the access panel sprang open and displayed the complex inner workings of the tree.

DESTRUCTION

Light spilled out from within. Taking hold of the turning mechanism, a few rotations was all it took for the massive entrance to open.

A strange blue-fluorescent light pierced the darkness. Quickly, the mechanism was reversed and the entrance closed. With a cry of determination, the sledgehammer rained blow upon blow on the tree's inner workings, shattering and destroying the pieces. Parts flew every which way. The energy that came with the adrenaline rush ebbed, and the hammer dropped to the ground. Satisfied that the tree would never open again, the magic lantern was hurled at the mechanism, shattering its glass lens. Exhausted, the job was done, and it was time for the journey home.

Chapter 19

INVERTED

J ake stared, stunned. She jumped backward and immediately everything changed; the tree's opaque entrance stood once more before her.

"No way," she mumbled.

She took a hesitant step forward again. The tree, the hill, the time rings in the meadow, they all had disappeared. Outer space surrounded her as she floated among the stars. There was no evidence of the hill or meadow she had left behind—no portal—just space. Looking below she gazed into the infinity of the universe.

It's another cavern.

But this one was different…upside down…inverted. Instead of a domed ceiling on which the night sky shone, in this cavern that existed below her, looking like a giant bowl. She seemed to be suspended near the top on an invisible catwalk.

Jake stood petrified. *Where does the catwalk begin and where does it end?* Dropping to her knees, she felt the smooth, glass-like surface. Her eyes adjusted, and she noticed the slight distortion of the stars made by the walkway—the width of the path was now obvious.

INVERTED

Jake stepped tentatively toward the center of the cavern where a pulsating column of light swirled brightly. It seemed alive…on guard… blue blobs danced about in amorphous yet ever changing shapes. She followed one such blob with her eyes as it darted and streaked to the top of the two-story ceiling where the column of light ended.

The invisibility of the entrance was worrisome, and Jake turned and retraced her steps to be certain it was still there. Six steps later she stood on the hill, the tree behind her.

This is weird. It's a different dimension or something.

Convinced that she could go in and out of the new tree at will, Jake returned inside to continue her search for Aaron. Maybe he was lost, unable to find his way out. Well she would not have that problem! She had a solution. Jake retrieved a small, green stuffed toy frog from her backpack and placed it on the catwalk, marking the exit. Out of habit she glanced around, embarrassed that someone might see her with such a toy. She took a step or two away from the stuffed animal and was convinced she would be able to spot it even in the darkness.

Marching forward, Jake kept her eyes locked on the walkway. As she neared the column of light, a couple of strands of hair that had escaped her braid were drawn toward it. Jake rubbed her arms as she felt goosebumps rise. A slight tingling vibrated under her skin—the air seemed charged with electricity.

The catwalk came to a fork in order to circle around the column of light.

Which way—left or right?

She decided to go left. The path narrowed. Sweat rolled down the back of her neck and into her shirt. She stopped, taking a moment to relax and gain her composure. Another path jutted out from the center. Was it the one she came in on? Had she gone all the way around?

Far behind and to the side of the light column, sat a well-lit area, like a small room that floated in the middle of space. From this distance, Jake could not make out any details. How could she have possibly missed that large bright object in the dark star field? Checking her bearings, she found the answer. The floating room was exactly opposite where she had entered, the light column had hidden it from view.

Multiple catwalks extended from the central light column like celestial wheel spokes. Where did they lead? Two of them she knew— one led to the way out and the other to the mysterious room. As for where the others went, she had no a clue. She hugged the path which circled the light column and sidestepped to the catwalk which led to the room.

Farther and farther she walked. The blackness folded in around her and she squinted so she could keep track of the walkway below. Thirty steps later, the room seemed no closer. Unlike the other cavern, which had its high decibel pounding vents, this one was eerily quiet.

Like space. She considered, thinking back to her science class. Mr. Thatcher, had explained that because space was a vacuum, no particles existed there. It was completely empty. Because sounds are made from vibrating particles, then there is nothing to vibrate in space and therefore no sound.

"How do astronauts hear one another in the space shuttle?" she had asked.

Mr. Thatcher had nodded admiringly. "Well does anyone know the answer," he asked the class. "Jacqueline asks a good question."

Jacqueline—he was the only teacher who still called her that. Usually on the first day of school she corrected the teachers during roll call. From that day forward they all called her Jake...except Mr. Thatcher. He refused no matter how many times she tried to correct him. He just stuck with Jacqueline.

Fortunately, Aaron was not in her class, otherwise she was sure he would have been the first to answer Mr. Thatcher's question. After a moment or two, no one piped in.

"Okay," Mr. Thatcher continued. "Even though space doesn't have any particles, the spaceship does! Think about it. How do the astronauts breathe?"

"Oxygen," someone murmured.

"Exactly," Thatcher exclaimed. "Ships are full of oxygen not to mention carbon dioxide that the astronauts breathe out. The inside of a spaceship is a particle-rich environment, so sound can travel as easily there as it does on earth."

"So," a boy from across the room had started, "I guess I get how they could hear each other. But how can we talk to them from earth? I mean, they can hear us and we can hear them over a radio. If you need particles for sound to travel, and there aren't any particles in space, how does the sound travel from the spaceship through empty space back to us on earth?"

Mr. Thatcher raised his eyebrows. "Also a good question, but it is slightly more complicated." He had paced to the front of the room. "You see sound isn't really going through space. Radio waves are, and they don't need particles. They travel through a vacuum just fine. For us to hear astronauts, their sound sort of hitches a ride on the radio waves."

Hitches a ride, Jake thought as she crossed high above the silent, star-filled basin. *I wonder where this ride is going to take me.* She neared her destination, but it was not really a room—rather it was a transparent platform which had widened into a large circular area with two semicircular control panels flanking the catwalk.

Bathed in light, the two panels were completely flat. Large, rectangular, black shapes were embedded on their sloped surfaces.

They looked like her grandmother's electric stove. A note was taped to one surface. She read the quickly scribbled words.

THIS WAY TO THE FUTURE!

The handwriting was unmistakable—it was her own.

Chapter 20
FEVER

Sunlight streamed through the schoolhouse windows, and Aaron shielded his eyes after waking from a restless night's sleep. He stretched his arms, which were sore from lying on the hard, wood-planked floor. Gingerly, he stood up. His cast complicated matters, but soon Aaron was moving about and loosening his muscles.

He opened the folded paper that held his pills from the apothecary, he took the aspirin and prayed for relief. His stomach growled—hungry again. As he took a seat at one of the many desks, the enormity of his situation sank in. He missed home. He missed his bed. He missed his own time. And though it was hard to admit—he missed his mom. He could not remember a time when his mother had not been there to help him when he was sick or hurt. Sure his dad was there too, but it was mom who made everything better. It was funny how much he had taken her for granted.

Choking back the tears, he wondered how he would get back home. The cavern was not working, he had lost the diary, and he was stuck in a time when aspirin was made to order. His only friend was an Amish boy, who he had known for a total of about two days. He had to admit that despite all his planning, this had not been on his contingency list.

What about Jake? Surely she had turned on the cavern and waited for him to emerge from the vortex. But clearly he would not be there if he could not get it to work in this time. What would she do?

She had been different because of the confidence she had gotten from the stupid diary. He almost preferred the "old Jake," who questioned his every move. The thing of it was that he actually liked it when she did that. It made him think about, and even change, his plans. Jake was smart, and frankly she made him better because of her challenges. He considered that maybe he had taken her friendship for granted as well.

Oh man, he thought, vigorously shaking his head. *I've got to snap out of it. I'm starting to think like a dumb greeting card or something.*

At that moment, he heard someone on the school's steps. There was no time to hide, especially slowed down by his leg. Whoever it was, he would have to try and come up with a convincing reason for him being there.

"Morning, Aaron," the Amish boy said as he entered. A gentle waft of air followed the boy in and Aaron caught a strong whiff of whatever his friend had been carrying in his hands. Aaron's stomach growled again, this time louder than the last.

"More scrapple?" Aaron asked.

"No," the boy replied. "But I know you will like it!"

The warmth of the breakfast coursed through Aaron as they two boys approached the forest from a completely different direction. He was not entirely sure what he had eaten, but it tasted similar to eggs and hash browns mixed with meat. Regardless, it was good, though it sat heavily in his stomach.

"What is it?" the boy asked.

"What do you mean?"

"Your face," the boy remarked. "You were thinking of something?"

"Well I was thinking how some things here are so different—especially the food."

"You do not eat eggs?"

"No it's not that," Aaron explained. "We don't eat that way every day. We are usually in a big rush to get to school. We have to pack our stuff, get dressed, brush our teeth, and get into the car. I usually just eat a bowl of Count Chocula on the way."

"Count who?"

"It's a breakfast cereal that comes in a box…oh never mind. It's difficult to explain."

As they walked, the Amish boy steadied him even though Aaron had mastered the use of the crutch even in the mucky, soft soil. As they approached the forest, they stopped to allow Aaron the opportunity to catch his breath.

"So, did you sleep well?" the boy asked.

"Honestly? Hardly at all," Aaron replied, moving his head from side to side and rolling it around in order to stretch his neck. "I slept on and off but my mind was racing."

"Racing?"

"Yeah, sorry. That means I had too many thoughts and they kept me awake. I couldn't figure out why the cavern wasn't working, and I wondered what Jake might be doing. Actually, I also had some thoughts about you."

"Me. What about me?"

"Well it's ironic that we have swapped places. You were in my time, alone, you didn't know anyone, and your family was long gone. Now here I am, also one hundred years from my own time. Maybe I'll get stuck here. Still, I do have a big advantage."

"What is that?"

"I know you. I don't know what I would have done without your help, especially with my leg." Aaron paused. He was not normally one to share his feelings—unless, of course, he was frustrated—then he showed them all too well. "Anyway, what I want to say is 'thank you.' Thank you for everything."

The Amish boy took the hand Aaron was offering and shook it vigorously while smiling. "No thanks are necessary. You are a friend. I would not be here if it were not for you."

They started walking once more through the field. "I was wondering about how you ended up in the cavern," Aaron said. "When I first moved into the farmhouse, Jake and I found a page of your diary inside an old trunk in the barn's hayloft. It was that page that began the whole journey for us."

"What was on the page?"

"That's exactly what I wanted to talk to you about. On one side was a diary entry. On it you mention hearing your name called on the wind."

Immediately, the Amish boy stiffened and stared ahead.

"Anyway," Aaron continued. "The same thing happened to me. I heard my name one night when I was camping. Later, I met Jake and she told me about a missing Amish boy, how my house was haunted, and blah, blah, blah. I thought it was you, of course, but now that you are back home, I'm not so sure. You obviously aren't missing anymore."

The boy looked bewildered. "I'm not sure I know what you are saying."

"Honestly, I'm not sure I know myself," Aaron said. "I haven't worked it through. Anyway, I do have an easier question."

FEVER

The Amish boy lifted his eyebrows. The expression was so unexpected that Aaron laughed out loud.

"What is it?"

"Sorry," Aaron said. "Sometimes you surprise me." Aaron decided not to explain and pressed on. "My question is, how did you find the tree? And when did you hear your name called on the wind? What happened?"

The boy answered cautiously. "I felt extremely ill one morning, and my mother had put me to bed to sleep off a high fever. She had placed cold cloths on my head, and replaced them when they got warm. She had opened my windows to get rid of 'the sick smell,' as she called it."

Aaron nodded, encouraging him to continue.

"I had been going in and out of sleep and had odd dreams. At some point, night came and a storm had rolled in. I had been awakened by a loud thunder clap. For a moment, I wasn't sure where I was. My room was dark. I heard the rain pelting the house and the sound of the wind whipping around and shaking the shutters."

Aaron watched fear register on the boy's face as he recounted the story.

"I remember rubbing my temples because my head pounded, and I shivered because of the cold breeze in the room. The covers were not enough to warm me, and a cold sweat made me feel hot and chilled at the same time. Exhausted I had finally gotten up to close the window. Rain spattered into the room, and I held out my hand for balance. As I shut the window, the wind howled and I had thought that I heard my name. I tilted my head to one side and concentrated. Lightning flashed and I searched the fields with blurry eyes, but honestly I could not see anything nor did I hear any more voices. Suddenly my door opened and my mother entered. Just then I had collapsed to the floor."

For a moment, Aaron had forgotten to breathe as he was enthralled by the exciting tale. "What happened then?" he asked.

"I must have passed out because the next thing I knew, I woke and it was morning. The storm had passed. My room was bright, and my window had been closed. The fever had broken, and I felt much better. I've often wondered if what happened had been a dream brought on by the fever."

The boy paused, turning to look directly at Aaron. "Then it happened again."

"What? What happened?" Aaron fought to keep up as the boy walked faster.

"This time it was not the wind. Whoever was calling, wanted me to know for sure that I was not imagining anything."

As the boy told his story Aaron recalled his own and remembered how frightened he had been the night he had found the old barn.

The boy continued. "A few days later, I was better and busy with my chores. I had forgotten the incident. I was plowing the fields near the creek that bordered the forest, and had felt like I was being watched."

As they walked, Aaron lost his balance and pitched forward, his crutch remained stuck in the mud. As he was about to land facedown in the muck, the boy pulled him with such force that Aaron thought his arm would be wrenched out of its socket.

"Are you okay?" the Amish boy asked.

"I think so." Aaron took a moment. He shook his arm and gingerly tested his leg. "Everything feels all right. I think my arm hurts more than anything else. You are really strong!"

The Amish boy smiled and blushed. "It is from my work in the fields."

Aaron liked seeing the boy this way. He was usually so serious and formal. It was good to know he could be a kid too.

"Okay, I think I'm good."

"Are you sure?" the boy asked.

"Well we're almost there. I can rest when we arrive. Let's give it a go!"

They resumed their march.

"I almost forgot! You were about to tell me what happened when you were plowing the fields."

"Yes. Near the forest, something had struck my side. At my feet, I saw a large rock. It could have only come from the forest. Walking in that direction, I found a drawing in the dirt on the other side of the creek."

"What?" Aaron exclaimed.

"I checked if anyone was nearby—but found no one. There was definitely no one in the fields. Whoever had thrown the rock had to be in the forest."

Aaron's brain raced as he tried to guess who it might have been or what they had been drawn. "Well—what was it? What was the picture of?"

"It was a map."

"A map to what?"

"At the time, I did not know. I ran home, got my diary, and brought it to the creek to copy the drawing. I realized it was a map to a tree."

Aaron's eyes grew wide.

"It is the same map from my diary."

Chapter 21
CHOICES

A chill ran through Jake. *How is this possible? Crazy time travel!* It had been weird enough seeing her handwriting in the Amish boy's diary, but this! It was incredible to find a note she had written in such a strange place. She had no memory of writing it. Aaron had tried to explain such things to her. He had said, "You'll write the diary entries in our future, which just happens to be in the past."

Right, like that made any sense.

"Obviously I've done it," she remembered saying while waving the book in his face. "It's right here."

"Well yes and no," he had replied.

"What do you mean by yes and no? Here it is—my handwriting. Are you telling me this isn't here?"

"No," he had explained. "What I'm saying is that it is there, but you haven't written it yet. That is why I said yes and no."

Jake remembered looking at him as if he were crazy. "Do you even hear the words coming out of your mouth?"

He started tapping his fingers on the table, and she sensed his frustration. A moment later his eyes brightened. "Okay," he had said.

"We'll go through an example." They had been hanging out in his room because a rainstorm had kept them inside. Aaron went to his desk, pulled open a drawer, and began rummaging. He had retrieved trading cards, erasers, old pens, toys from discarded happy meals, an old cell-phone power cord, and finally found what he was looking for. "Got it!"

"Post-It notes?" Jake asked.

"Yeah, you'll see." He grabbed one of the many pencils that were now strewn about, and went over to the wall opposite from where she sat. "What was the first thing you did today?"

"I don't know—wake up I guess."

"Great." He took the first Post-It and wrote, "Got Up" in big letters with a "#1" written on top. "I'm going to place these notes on the wall in the order you did them."

Jake continued describing her day's activities, and Aaron numbered and placed them in order on the wall.

#1 Got Up
#2 Had Breakfast
#3 Milked the Cow
#4 Cleaned Room
#5 Did Homework
#6 Ate Snack
#7 Did Laundry
#8 Had Lunch
#9 Rode Bike

"Let's switch it up." He picked up Post-It #5. Let's say after you cleaned your room, you decide to go back in time to when you were sleeping. In other words, before you got up." He placed #5 before #1.

"Now after you finish your homework, you return by traveling forward in time to the place right before you left. Then you continue on. You eat the snack, do the laundry, blah, blah, blah."

"What's the point?"

"The point is," Aaron continued, "when you wake up, your homework would already be done, even though you haven't done it yet. You still have to have breakfast, milk the cow, and clean your room before you go back in time and do your homework. That is why you see your homework done when you wake up, but you don't have any memory of doing it because you haven't done it yet!"

It sort of made sense, but she was still trying to sort things out. "If I find my homework already done, why would I go back and do it? How would I even know to go back in time? What if I don't and instead go straight to eating the snack'? How would my homework get done?"

"You've got it!"

Aaron started moving the Post-It notes around. "You see, with time travel, you can completely change the order, but the problem is exactly as you said. If you do change the order, for example, seeing your homework finished before you've even done it, it could change what you do in the future. What would happen if you decided never to go back in time? Does the homework disappear? Would you even know it disappeared because having skipped going back in time, you would never have seen the completed homework when you got up. That is why I don't want to read the diary—it could influence what we do and change everything. We can't risk it!"

"Honestly, you lost me," she had said, staring at the wall of yellow stickies.

Now staring at the note on the control panel in this strange new cavern, she accepted the fact that sometime in *her* future she would write and leave this note on the console sometime in the past. When and why, she was not sure about. It was yet another mystery.

Smooth, black, and reflective, the control console had no markings. *Well*, Jake thought. *It must be safe. I've obviously touched it before, the note proves that. I might as well try it.* Jake reached forward. For some reason she expected the surface to be cold, instead it radiated warmth. Quickly she touched a finger to the surface, as if testing a hot stove. Almost immediately, the console came to life. Colors, dials, and pictures appeared but unlike a computer screen, these images were projected three dimensionally within the console.

On the left side of the display, an image of a giant spoked wheel emerged. Squinting and bringing her face closer to the console, she hovered a hand over the image. The wheel came to life and spun, responding to the movement of her hands. She found she could zoom in and out, rotate the image, and focus in on any area. It was then she noticed one of the spokes had a segment marked in blue on one end. Curious, she touched the blue area. Suddenly a section from across the cavern brightened.

Jake carefully walked away from the control platform to investigate. The light came from the entrance. The walkway leading back to the meadow was now illuminated, her green stuffed frog was clearly visible.

Returning to the control panel, she touched the end of another spoke. The previous blue area dimmed and another lit up. Inside the cavern, the entrance walkway faded to darkness and another path brightened.

Nodding to herself she understood—the image on the screen represented the cavern. It controlled the different paths leading out from the central light column. Other than turning the lights for the paths on and off, she had no idea what else the controls did or where the paths led.

A sphere-shaped object filled the second half of the display. It looked like a large, clear ball with tiny lights surrounding the surface. When she touched the different spokes on the left-hand side, and lit the paths around the cavern, the pattern on the sphere changed. At the same time, the star field below her also changed.

Wait a minute, she thought.

She illuminated the spoke control that corresponded to the entrance. Jake moved her hand over the sphere's image and found she could rotate and move the sphere. As she did, the star field below her moved in concert with the image on the screen.

This is like the other cavern's lever controls.

Moving the slider bar underneath the sphere caused the ball to focus on specific stars or move away from them. Scanning the deepest part of the cavern below the platform, she located the red targeting circle.

It's the same, just inverted.

The pieces fell into place. She re-read the note on the console.

THIS WAY TO THE FUTURE!

Jake had a feeling of déjà vu. When had she seen this before?

The diary! *That's it!*

She pulled out the journal and flipped to the page she had been looking at back in the cavern. There it was. The words "Future" and "Inverted" were written at the top and bottom of the page. The picture made sense now. The drawing of the tree—and the big curve that looked like a bowl underneath—had to be this new cavern.

And what about the phrase, "Not the moon setting"? Its big block capital letters were identical to how she had written this note on the console.

Maybe the two go together!

Not the Moon Setting This Way to the Future

Could it be that the other cavern was the way to the past, but this one was the way to the future?

Released from its perch, the maple leaf wafted skyward, riding the updraft through the forest. It tumbled and twisted as the breeze softened. The leaf floated, swaying side-to-side like an abandoned park swing. Finally it landed on its side, but it did not rest. Once more it took flight and hovered over the ground, tripping and falling over the rocks and twigs that littered the ground. At last it came to rest in the rustling stream.

Once a bird in flight, the leaf was now a boat that floated downstream. Onward it went, riding the stream like a white-water kayaker. Expertly it surfed, dodging pebbles and weaving through debris. Once it found a clear path the leaf accelerated rapidly, until it encountered a green tube snaked in the stream. Here the leaf became wedged against a rock.

The current pushed on the leaf, which fluttered in frustration as it attempted to release itself from the grip of the rock. The more it struggled, the more stuck the leaf became. Suddenly a hand grabbed the leaf and tossed it aside. Wet and soggy from its travels, the lone maple leaf stuck to the dirty bank of the stream and watched as the hand lifted the rock and removed the green tube trapped beneath.

THE INVERTED CAVERN

The hose was tossed aside over the bank. Water flowed out and a gurgling sound erupted from its end as the once engorged hose filled with air. The owner of the hand walked away, laughing.

⤬

Back inside the cavern, the console blinked and caught Jake's attention. Looking at the wheel spokes on the left side of the screen, Jake saw the flashing blue tip of the entrance path. She touched the screen's location, but the blinking continued. Curious, she walked to the edge of the platform and inspected the star field below. It was the same as the sphere on the right side of the display, but the flashing continued.

What's going on?

Deciding to investigate, Jake made her way back to the entrance. She returned the stuffed frog to her pack and checked her watch. Two hours had gone by. It would be best if she left, collected her thoughts, made a plan, and then returned. As if in agreement, her stomach growled.

"Okay, okay, we can go," she said, laughing to herself. The snacks she had brought were gone. Nothing less than a full meal would appease her hunger now. Before leaving, she turned toward the pulsating column and admired the wondrous new cavern. Shaking her head, she wondered how and why it was created. Better yet, by whom?

Maybe we'll never know.

With that, she marched forward to the exit.

Five steps later, she was still walking.

Ten steps.

No exit.

The central column was farther away than ever.

CHOICES

Nervous heat rose from her skin.

The portal should have been here. This is the right path, I'm certain of it.

Holding her hand out in front, she continued walking forward, waiting to reach the hill at any moment. As she continued her virtual space walk, she noticed the stars projected on the deep and dark cavern below became closer and closer to the catwalk.

Why are the stars coming closer? A step later, her hand touched a wall.

Dead end. She had reached the far side of the cavern.

It can't be! she thought, her anxiety building.

The wall was solid and as cold and smooth as granite. She pounded her fists, then felt up, down, and side-to-side. But the surface always felt the same way. She touched the place where the catwalk terminated into the wall and found nothing—no portal—no way out—nothing. Something had happened, and it must be related to the blue flashing light on the console.

Jake heard rattling behind her, and she was startled. Quickly she turned around but saw nothing.

"Who's there?" she yelled. There was no reply, but no matter which way she faced, the sound always came from directly behind her.

Then she realized what it was—it was her. Her body shook so hard that the contents in her backpack rattled.

I'm trapped.

Chapter 22
DISCOVERY

What do you mean it's the same map from your diary?" Aaron asked.

"I was afraid that rain or an animal would ruin the map, so I captured it in my diary. It was the place where I kept my most precious thoughts, prayers, instructions my father had given me on shucking corn or shoeing a horse. I don't know what it is like for you, but we only use paper for our most important documents. My diary was my one luxury, and the map...well, it seemed important."

"What did you do then? Did you find the tree?"

The boy shook his head. "After I copied the map, I checked to make sure everything was correct, then I brushed away the dirt, rocks, and sand, erasing any trace of it."

"What? Why?"

"I had already copied it, and a part of me believed it was just a joke."

Aaron thought back to his experience at the tanning salon. The bed's UV light had brought forth the faded image from the diary page. The map had started from drawings in the dirt—from low tech to high tech. Ironic. But the map Aaron remembered had more than just directions drawn on it.

"Was there anything else drawn in the sand?" Aaron asked.

"What do you mean?"

"Like pictures of gears or instructions, you know, information on how to open the tree, that kind of thing?"

"No, nothing more. There was just the map."

Aaron wondered how the additional information got on the page. *Maybe that part hasn't happened yet.*

Aaron was not certain what to do next. His anxiety had risen throughout the night and the next morning. He had thought through some experiments they could use to try to determine why the moon setting had not worked. Figuring that out was the key to getting him home. At the same time he could not deny that he had grossly miscalculated how difficult time travel could be. Maybe he would never make it back to the future and would stay trapped in the past.

Perhaps, that was why he risked sending the diary forward. Maybe he wanted to change history because he had gotten trapped. He clearly should have thought this through more. Somehow, Jake's confidence in the diary had made him confident as well. After all, they had written notes in the diary, so he assumed everything would be fine. But he had not considered the writing could have occurred if they were both trapped back in time.

Jake's writing, he thought. That part did not make sense. Sure, he was back one hundred years, unable to use the moon setting and trapped, but Jake was still back in their time. He was certain she would never come back alone…unless…unless something went wrong in the future. He shook his head.

Everything would be okay as long as Jake stayed put. He turned his attention back to the Amish boy.

"What happened next?" Aaron asked. "You found the map and copied it. I take it you found the tree, but how did you open it? The map only marked an X and didn't even show the tree. We searched and searched for anything that could be worthy of an X." Aaron thought back to the time when he and Jake scoured the forest. It was only because of a fall, while racing down the tree, that they scratched away the bark and found the hidden panel. It was really just an accident that they even found the cavern.

"I never thought of that," the Amish boy said pensively.

"Hadn't thought of what?"

"It was always obvious to me that the X indicated the tree."

Aaron waited for the boy to explain.

"You see, I still don't know who it was."

Aaron furrowed his brow. *This must be how Jake feels when I'm thinking something through. No wonder she gets frustrated with me.* "You're not making any sense. Please back up and tell me what happened."

"Well, I followed the directions on the map. I had never crossed the stream into the forest before that. I'm not sure why. It was one of those things that no one talked about but all the kids understood we were to stay away."

Like when I moved in, Aaron thought. But in his time it made sense because of the legend of the missing boy. Here, there was no such mystery. Or was there? Was there an even older story that went with the forest? He decided to ask. "What do you mean you understood to stay away?"

The boy removed his hat and finger-combed his matted hair. "I'm not sure I can explain. It was a subject that everyone avoided. Sometimes a younger child, who didn't know any better, would ask about the forest and he would be quickly hushed by an adult. Concerned looks would pass from face to face around the room. It was what was not said that made the point."

Aaron understood. He could often tell when his mother was in a bad mood even if she did not say anything. Strange. Was it possible to actually feel someone else's mood? And if everyone felt the same way about a place, could you feel that mood if you went there?

"So anyway, I knew I should not go, but the rock must have been thrown from the forest, and that was where the map pointed to, so I crossed the creek and entered. Once I came to the place that was marked with the X on the map, it was clear that the tree was what had been indicated."

"How so?"

"Because, Aaron. The tree was already open."

"Open?" Aaron's mind reeled. Whoever had spoken his name, thrown the rock, and drawn the map, had to be the same person who left the tree open for the boy to find. But who could it be? Aaron never considered that someone else knew the secrets of the time cavern.

"Yes, when I got there, I found the hidden notch in the tree already open and the lever connected. The gears had been turned and the doorway leading into the tree was open."

"And you went in?" Aaron remembered his arguments with Jake, and the wrangling they went through before deciding it was safe to enter. He was stunned the boy would venture in alone.

"Actually, I didn't go in. I thought it was unwise to enter and wanted to confide in someone. I decided to tell Sarah. She was someone I could trust and I needed her help. So I walked back to—"

Aaron wondered why the boy abruptly stopped his story.

"No, no, no it cannot be it cannot be..." the boy yelled, shaking his head as he ran forward through the forest.

Aaron followed as fast as he could and found the boy kneeling on the ground in front of their tree, studying pieces of something. As he approached, he realized what they were.

"It's ruined," the boy said, holding the broken gears and nodding toward the vandalized tree. "We'll never be able to get into the tree now. What will we do?"

Surveying the damage, Aaron saw something he thought he had lost. He picked up the bent and broken tube that had made the journey through time unlike the diary.

"What is that?" the boy asked, seeing Aaron inspected it.

"It's my flashlight. Someone else definitely knows about the cavern, and they don't want me going home."

Chapter 23

HERE AND THERE

Her chest heaved, and the breaths came fast and furious. Her thoughts raced as fast as her heart. Turning, she walked back toward the center light column.

This is crazy, she thought. *I know I came in this way. I must have changed the entrance when I was fiddling with the control panel. The blue light must be an indicator, a warning perhaps. I'm sure of it. I have to undo whatever I did!*

She left the catwalk and stepped onto the central hub which led around to the control panel but stopped short. Once more, she set the stuffed frog on the path that led to where the exit had been. *Don't want to mess this up.*

Once back at the controls, Jake manipulated the images on the spoke and wheel portion of the panel. Like before, she could turn each of the catwalk's lights on and off.

Wait a minute. When I came in, the catwalk I was on had been dark. Maybe that's what's wrong.

She turned off the lights, except for the control platform, and maneuvered the star field to the same conditions as when she had entered the cavern.

Convinced that everything was in the state it had been, including the placement of the note—her note—on the panel, she returned back the way she had come.

This time she left the stuffed frog as a marker, losing it would not matter if she could find the way out. Her lips tightened and she focused on walking across the invisible bridge. A few steps later she shrugged her shoulders in defeat. It did not work. The portal out was gone.

Sitting cross-legged, she examined the diary, hoping for a clue—any clue—of what else she could try. All she kept coming back to was that the moon setting was not the way to the future. The word "inverted" kept nagging at her mind. She had learned it from her "words of the day" calendar, a Christmas gift that was perfectly timed for the start of a new year. Her mother, who had been a former high school English teacher, had given it to her.

Her mother took every opportunity to correct Jake's grammar and help improve her vocabulary. "If you don't know *exactly* what a word means, don't use it!" she would say. Her mother frequently discussed word roots.

"Most are from Latin, which is a dead language." Seeing the confused look on Jake's face, her mom explained. "A dead language is one that is no longer spoken as a native language."

"That doesn't make any sense, Mom," Jake had said.

"Why do you say that?"

"Because if what you say is true, many of the words we speak in English have Latin roots. Spanish, Portuguese, French, and Italian all descended from Latin, so we essentially speak Latin every day."

Her mother smiled and Jake beamed. "Very good point, dear. I suppose it is a matter of perspective." Later her mother had given her the calendar, which provided a new word each day. Jake studied their meaning and roots. After she learned a new word, she underlined it in red in an old unabridged dictionary. Her goal was to have them all underlined one day. Although she had never counted them, she knew from the Internet that there were at least 250,000 words in the English language but most people only knew twenty- to thirty-thousand. Unfortunately, without using those words every day, she forgot many of them.

But she did remember "inverted." It is an adjective that indicates that top and bottom have been reversed. This cavern was the reverse of the original cavern she and Aaron had found. If that were true, perhaps the different star settings would dictate how far you went into the future, instead of the past. Perhaps the light column in the middle was the portal to these different times.

Jake shook her head vigorously. *No*—she could not imagine leaping into the future. There had to be another way out. That option would be a last resort. Before going there she needed to explore the other spokes leading from the center. They must have some purpose—some destination. But what was it? and where did they go?

Taking a couple of steps on a new path, Jake walked slowly, not wanting to suddenly pop through another invisible exit which might leave her stranded. She moved as if she were blindfolded while playing a game of Pin the Tail on the Donkey; her hands reached out, feeling for something that was not there. Soon she was far from the light column and found the outer wall of the cavern once more. Doubling back, she repeated this three more times—every path ended the same way—in a dead end. There was no way in and no way out, except possibly...

Okay, let's think this through, she considered. *I've tried everything and I know I must have found a way out because at some point, I'm going to write the note left here on the console.*

At least that was what she hoped. Aaron was always warning her about changing the past, but what about changing the future? Since the note was still there, she felt that it indicated she was definitely going to write it. Though a convincing argument intellectually, it did not provide much comfort. In any case, she knew what she had to do—she had to go into the future.

Studying the star field, Jake recognized many constellations, especially her favorite, Orion. But those stars would not work. The ones in Orion's belt were more than seven hundred light years away. If the cavern worked the way she thought it did, that would mean leaping seven hundred years into the future. *No way!*

The star she wanted was much closer. In fact, it was next to the sun, and she remembered it was the closest star to earth—Proxima Centauri—it was just a little more than four light years away. If for some reason she could not find a way back in time and got stuck in the future, it would only be four years from her own time. Her friends, family, and everything else would still be around—even if they would be a little older.

She operated the virtual star sphere on the console, and the star field below spun at her command. Somewhat disoriented by the cosmic motion in her peripheral vision, Jake caught herself from falling. *Maybe I should go a little slower...*

Finally she spotted the star. Jake was uncertain how to focus on it, so she did the only thing that made sense. She pointed at the star and pushed at the console. Immediately, the chamber zoomed in, and locked on it with a red target indicator. For a moment Jake thought the light pattern in the central column had changed—first the swirling pattern seem to freeze, which was followed by a quick one, two, three pulse, then everything was back to normal.

I can't believe I'm about to do this. Jake's muscles tensed. She racked her mind for an alternative but none came. As she looked at the note on the console, she found herself frustrated with its brevity and wondered why the heck she had not left a better clue. *Why aren't there more instructions?*

Taking a piece of paper from her backpack, she scribbled a note that detailed what had happened in the chamber: the blue lights on the display, how she got trapped, her belief that the beam of light was the portal to the future, and her plan to go there by setting the cavern to four years.

"There!" She slapped down the note in plain view. No one could possibly miss this. "Enough of these cryptic, half-baked messages! Besides, I'm not sending the note into the future. It's staying here, so I can't change the past." Even as the words came out of her mouth, she was not sure they made any sense. But saying them with conviction, and a stern head nod, made her feel better.

When she turned to face the column, her shoulders slumped. "So much for conviction," she said aloud.

"C'mon, Jake. Hold it together." She tried to cheer herself up. *Maybe I should run straight into it without hesitating—just get it over with.*

She chuckled.

Who was she kidding? She could not even do that at a swimming pool. Others had always made fun of her because of her hesitation. While they would simply run and jump in, submerging their entire bodies all at once, Jake would descend a bit at a time. First she put her ankles in, then her knees, then waist, and so on. *If I can't jump into a pool, I'm certainly not going to take the plunge when time traveling!*

The swirling light danced across the stuffed frog standing guard on the opposite side of the hub. The side of Jake's mouth curled into a smile at the irony of this simple little toy sitting amid the complexity of what surrounded her. Giving a wink to the animal, she scrutinized the light column. Wisps of luminescent fog took shape and faded, replaced by another morphing mist which soon dissipated.

"Okay, keep breathing, Jake." Her hand penetrated the column's outer boundary, and she was immediately wrenched into the light. She wanted to yell but could not. Suspended in the column, Jake was frozen in time.

The cavern hummed with the low vibration of a large generator. Within the milky haze the air charged, and the tiny hairs on her arms and the back of her neck stood on end. The generator sound intensified and a series of plasma-ball, lightning streams electrified the cavern. Paralyzed, Jake watched as her hands faded. The charge increased, and Jake's body glowed from within as it slowly disintegrated into a mist. She became part of the fog, joining with the swirling mass in the light column as the eddy current dissipated. The plasma streams stopped, the generator sound quieted, and Jake was no more.

Chapter 24
BORN IN A BARN

A aron bounced on the ladder.

"What are you doing?" the Amish boy asked as he placed the last of the broken pieces onto the workbench.

"It's weird to see how sturdy the barn is. I'm used to seeing it in my time with missing boards, holes in the roof, rotted wood—it's completely dilapidated. When I first climbed this ladder, I thought it would collapse."

"Imagine how it was for me!" the boy said, adjusting his suspenders. "When I was in your time, the barn was a reminder of what I had lost. A part of me did not want to believe what was happening. I wanted it all to be some type of strange dream, but the barn was proof. Everything was old, run down and dead—like my family and friends. I was alone and afraid, but then you and your friend saved me. Now it is my turn to return the favor. We *will* find a way to get you back."

Rummaging through the pile of junk that had been the tree's gears, the boy shook his head. "But now, I don't know what to do. I thought it would be difficult when we could still get inside the cavern, but now..." He gestured to the pile.

As Aaron listened to the boy, he noticed a small, half-completed wooden rocking horse on the workbench. "I can't believe it," he said. "This was *supposed* to happen. I mean *it is* happening the way it is supposed to. At least I think it is…"

"What do you mean?"

Aaron joined him at the bench, and snatched up a tool. "This here. It's a chisel, right? And here is a hand drill, and saws, of course. Everything is all here."

"What is all here?" The boy was animated now. "Please, Aaron what are you talking about?"

"You know how to use these tools, right? I mean you're good at woodworking and such? You are the one building this rocking horse, aren't you?"

"I suppose," the boy admitted, his cheeks reddening.

Aaron took ahold of the horse and admired the details. "How did you learn to do this? It's amazing."

"My father taught me." The boy went to the side of the bench and picked out a piece of wood. "This is one of the first good pieces I made."

The boy handed it to Aaron who received it skeptically. To him, it looked like a simple piece of wood, an inch thick and about two feet long. Its four sides tapered on one end.

"It's the leg for a table," the boy explained. "While it may not look like much, the challenge is making the taper on each side equal. My hands were blistered by the time I finished that. In my first few attempts, I had the blade on the planer too long and it gouged too much wood." He hung his head. "I was in too much of a hurry."

Aaron raised an eyebrow, appreciating the result. The piece was clean and uniform—very professional.

"This piece taught me a lot about woodworking. You see, I tried to force too much in my first attempts. To make it correctly, you need to pay attention to the wood's grain. The striations from a tree's growing rings will affect the strength and uniformity of the piece and how it will wear over time. First you have to find the right piece of wood, then cutting, planing, sanding, and refining become a labor of love. Only then will you make something correctly. Carpentry requires careful observation and knowing what a piece can, and cannot, do."

Aaron nodded.

"My father says life is the same way," the boy continued. "He told me god gave me two eyes and two ears for observation and a brain to take into consideration the feelings of others. He said I should listen more than I talk."

Aaron thought about his own dad. He also said stuff like that. Not quite the same way, but it was the same message. How did dads know these things? Was there a universal "dad book"?

The boy continued reciting, "Patience, planning, detail, and persistence are the keys to success." Taking the piece back from Aaron, he admired it.

"Are you working on the rest of the table?" Aaron asked. "When will you add this leg?"

The boy stared in disbelief. "Aaron, there is no table. I keep this piece as a reminder of these lessons."

What a different world, Aaron thought. Maybe life was too easy in the twenty-first century. A machine could create a perfect table leg in just minutes—and no life lesson would come from it.

The Amish boy interrupted Aaron's thoughts. "What I don't understand is why you have such an interest in my woodworking skills."

"Right, I can't believe we got so far off track." Aaron seized a shattered gear retrieved from the tree. "You are going to rebuild the broken parts—using wood!"

"What? I'm not that good!"

"Yes you are," Aaron replied, separating the pieces into piles. "In my time, you've already done it! Jake and I found the gears you made in your keepsake chest. Back in my time, the tree only worked with replacement parts. We wondered where they came from and why they were made out of wood. Now we know! Everything is happening according to some master plan: me coming back, losing the flashlight, the tree's destruction, it all fits!"

The Amish boy took two severely bent disfigured gears and held them up. "I am glad you are happy about this, Aaron. But I am the one who has to duplicate these complex pieces. If I understand these parts correctly, the teeth of one gear must mesh with the gaps in the others." The boy tested combinations of pieces on the workbench and shook his head.

"What's wrong?" Aaron asked.

"Each piece has to be perfect for them to fit together. It would be challenging enough with two gears, but there are too many parts. Plus," he said, displaying an odd-shaped object, "there are other parts that I have no idea what they do."

"It's okay. You can do it." Aaron placed his hand on the boy's shoulder, and gave him a squeeze. "I *know* you can. Don't worry about what the parts do, just duplicate them as closely as you can. After all, we managed to get you back home even though we didn't know exactly how the cavern works!"

"Yes, and look where that has gotten us! You are trapped here." He shook his head. "But something still troubles me more than any of this."

"What is that?"

"We don't know who did this. Who destroyed these parts, and why? It would appear that someone is trying to stop us."

BORN IN A BARN

The Amish boy had a point. Solving the moon setting problem was difficult enough. Having someone trying to hinder their progress, added a significant wrinkle to the mix. "It's strange, and I think you are right, someone is probably working against us. But keep in mind that someone also made the map for you to find the tree, and left the entrance open so we have someone helping us as well. There must be more than one person at work here."

I wish I could hear what they are saying, Samuel thought as he stared through the eye-level knot hole near the back of the barn. He had stood motionless for at least fifteen minutes, and now massaged his legs to work out the cramps. His irritation rose as the dank smell of impending rain mixed with the thick odors from the animals. It was time to leave and start the long walk home.

Chapter 25

OUT OF THE FOG

The fog swirled thick in her dream. It had felt so real. Jake brushed away the condensation from her cheek and realized she was no longer paralyzed and she had not been dreaming after all.

Nothing lay beyond the haze of the cloud that enveloped her. The lightning streams had stopped and the generator hum was gone. Quickly, she felt her arms, legs, and torso, checking to make sure they were all there.

Alive! But trapped?

Waving at the air, she struggled to see. She walked forward, hands outstretched. A twig snapped beneath her foot. The ground was uneven. The air smelled earthy and a light breeze blew across her face.

I'm outside.

Memories flooded back about being trapped in the cavern. She had been frozen in the light column, surrounded by lightning, but had felt no pain. She now felt nothing, except the numbness and tingling from the electricity, which reminded her of a science museum field trip.

During the long winter months, Jake's school arranged for field trips to get the kids out and about. The science museum was housed inside a renovated mansion named after a local entrepreneur—Ester Braken. Ms. Bracken had wanted to give back to the community, so she had created the museum, which fascinated everyone who visited. Jake remembered standing in a circle with her classmates surrounding a woman dressed in what looked like a blue flight attendant's uniform. Above them, a stained glass ceiling cast a beautiful array of colored lights around the room. Standing on a raised stage, the woman had described the experiment they were about to perform.

"What do you think that tall thing underneath the sheet next to her is?" Aaron had whispered.

"Shh! Be quiet and listen!" Jake had admonished.

The woman frowned in their direction and then continued. "You've probably heard the stories about Benjamin Franklin tying a key to a kite and flying it during a thunderstorm." She waited for a response from the class but saw only an occasional nod. "Well he was fascinated by electricity. He even held static electricity parties! His guests were given glass rods and were taught to rub them against wool, after which they were able to make small scraps of paper dance!"

"Great party," Aaron had said, but Jake gave him the stink eye.

"They also made their hair stand on end. Has anyone here ever taken a balloon and rubbed it on your head to do the same thing?" the woman asked.

A few hands went up.

"That is a static electricity game."

"Sounds boring," another kid shouted, and Aaron gave Jake a superior look.

"Well, you have to remember, there wasn't any television or other types of electronics to play with. But what if I could show you a way to not only make your hair stand on end, but also use static electricity to create sparks and lightning bolts? Does that sound like more fun?"

The woman swept back the cloth and revealed a machine that looked like it was straight out of an old black-and-white late-night TV horror movie. The machine was about three feet tall and had a large aluminum sphere about the size of a beach ball mounted on top a plastic tube. At the bottom of the tube, wires came out and connected a motor housed inside a Plexiglas box. On top of the glass box was what looked like a rubber mat.

"I've got to make me one of those," Aaron had said, poking Jake with his elbow.

"Class, this is a Van de Graaff generator. Inside this tube is a big belt powered by the motor below. The belt moves across material much like Ben Franklin's guests had brushed their glass rod over wool, but this machine creates a lot more static electricity. The belt collects and deposits the static charge on this metal ball at the top. The motor keeps it going and going. In fact, it can generate thousands and thousands of volts—way more than this little nine volt battery."

Passing the small battery around the room, one of the children asked, "Is that safe? My parents are always telling me to be careful around electricity."

"Your parents are right to warn you. Electricity can be *very* dangerous, especially if you don't know what you are doing. Even though we are creating huge amounts of voltage, it is still safe because the current is actually very low."

The kids returned puzzled looks.

"It is the amount of current that harms people, differences in voltage is not a problem if the current is small," she clarified.

After the motor engaged, the kids heard a low hum. The woman pressed a remote and the room went dark. The multicolored lights shining through the stained glass remained the only illumination. Taking a wand with a small metal ball on one end, she held it near the machine. Suddenly a tiny blue lightning bolt jumped from the big metal ball to her wand.

The class had gasped and Jake had involuntarily grabbed Aaron's arm.

For the next experiment, the woman placed foil bowls upside down on the machine. When the generator was turned on, the bowls flew like Jiffy Pop spaceships. One of the coolest experiments involved a fluorescent light tube. Holding it in her bare hands, it lit up when the woman moved it toward the generator!

"Amazing!" Aaron had said.

"Okay class," the woman had said as she placed her toys on the bench. "I need a volunteer for the last demonstration, preferably someone with long hair."

Before Jake knew it Aaron had pushed her forward and lifted her arm from behind.

"Great," the woman had said, "come on up."

Embarrassed, but not wanting to chicken out in front of the entire class, Jake stepped forward. The woman had her stand on the mat covering the Plexiglas-encased motor. Jake grimaced with concern.

"It's okay, honey," she had whispered in Jake's ear. "You won't get a shock. The rubber mat you are standing on will protect you."

She took Jake's right hand, placed it on the metal sphere, and started the device. "Pay attention everyone, the charge that normally is placed on this ball is now going to travel to…what's your name?"

"Jake," she heard herself say sheepishly, feeling her face redden.

"The charge will now travel through Jake's hand, into her body and charge her hair."

Even as the woman explained this, Jake's skin had begun to crawl. The woman undid Jake's braid and her hair stuck straight out. The class laughed, and Jake noticed many looked jealous, probably because they wished they had volunteered.

Going into the light column had felt similar to when she had been in the Van de Graaff generator experiment, except this time was much more intense—almost as if she had changed from matter to energy. For the moment, Jake was just happy to be alive. Taking a cautious step, Jake saw that the fog was lifting, and the sun was starting to poked through the haze.

Brushing aside a low-hanging branch, Jake walked out of the forest. The fog rolled over the flat fields and was thicker near the sound of a small bubbling stream.

The creek!

Turning to face the forest, she knew where she was.

I made it! It worked!

Jake hugged herself, scrunching up her shoulders as warmth spread through her body. She would be okay and all her tension and anxiety released with a sigh. She had done it. She had found a way out all by herself. All she needed to do now was get her bearings and find the tree then she could reset the cavern and pop back to her time. Voila!

She checked the extra helium canisters she had packed before starting this journey. At the time, she had no idea if she would need them, but Aaron always had lots of crazy stuff in his backpack, and that taught her it was best to be prepared. Especially with items that would be pretty hard to find. After all, it had taken them quite a bit of work to obtain the helium to unlock the tunnel the first time. They had eventually used helium balloons from school. Jake smiled at the memory of escaping from school with a trash bag full of balloons. Looking back, she could not believe they had actually pulled it off.

Jake looked at the position of the sun. It was already late afternoon, but it felt more like early morning. The fog had cleared significantly, and it was gone by the time she arrived at the tree. Opening the notch, Jake wondered how they could have ever missed the secret compartment. Peering inside, she froze.

"Oh, no!"

The gears were gone! But where could they be?

As soon as she asked the question, the answer came to her. Of course, they had to be in the trunk back in Aaron's barn. She would quickly sneak to the farm, take the gears, and head back to the tree.

As she walked, she replayed Aaron's warnings about not changing the past in her head and wondered if it was possible to change the future. Was that even a possibility? Once she found the gears, she would put them in the tree, open the cavern, and travel back to her own time. But then would she end up changing the future? She would be moving the gears from the trunk to the tree. Aaron and her future self would find the gears missing and have no idea what had happened to them. Would that change the future? And even if it did, would it matter since the future had not happened yet?

Then a crazy thought hit her. Maybe the past and future were forever connected. If time was like a book that had already been written from beginning to end, then time traveling could simply be like opening the book to different pages. After experiencing a few pages, the traveler could close the book and open it at a completely different page forward or backward but the story would never change.

When Jake had read, *A Wrinkle In Time*, she had done just that.

She had found it among many of the books that her mother had collected. For years the books had been stored in old moving boxes, but one day her father had created a reading room by constructing floor-to-ceiling shelves along one wall of their den. Her mom had proudly displayed the books and one had caught Jake's eye. The cover showed a picture of three kids floating in space surrounded by radiating circles. She was not a big reader or science fiction buff, but she had opened the book to the middle and read a few pages.

Immediately she had been drawn to the main characters—especially Meg Murray. In some ways, she thought of herself as Meg. Jumping to another section of the book, Jake read about someone named Mrs. Whatsit. Each section she had read was fascinating, but it did not make much sense as she was getting the story in bits and pieces. Eventually, she read the entire book starting from page one, and as the story unfolded, the context of the small snippets she previously read made sense.

Maybe time travel was the same way. Could the whole book of life already be written? All of human history—the whole thing?

Jake shook her head. *I've been hanging around Aaron too long.* The fact is she needed to get home, and she would do anything to get there. So she would move a couple of gears—that would not change the fate of the universe. It might be confusing for their future selves, but they were smart. They would figure it out.

Jake scanned the horizon, and was close enough now to see the farm. Clear as day she saw Aaron's house and a new-looking van sitting on the long dirt driveway. The old faded swing set his younger brothers had played on was still there, but a new flower garden bordered one end of the house. Unfortunately that was not the only thing that had changed. To the south of the house, where the old Amish barn should have been, only a cleared space and a tractor stood.

The barn, the hayloft, and the chest were gone.

Chapter 26

STOLEN!

Reaching behind his back, Aaron rolled to his side and removed a large piece of straw and threw it across the stall. Sunlight streamed into the barn and the smell of sweaty animals and wet hay filled his nose. Massaging his stiff muscles, he was surprised how well he had slept.

The irony of the situation came upon him quickly. Here he was trapped one hundred years from his own time, sleeping the night away in a barn and wondering if he would make it home. A few short weeks ago, the Amish boy had been in Aaron's place.

What was I thinking? Who cared what was in the dumb diary? Just because we saw our handwriting doesn't mean I had to come back so quickly—or even at all. I could have chosen never to come. Then again, maybe he could not.

Everything had turned out fine for the Amish boy. He made it home unharmed. With Jake's help, Aaron had solved that mystery, found the missing helium bottles, and learned the secrets of the cavern. Why did he have to press their luck? He knew better than most the dangers of traveling through time—after all, he was the one constantly warning Jake. Yet, he had come back. *What was I thinking?*

Even as he thought about this, the answer came to him, and it was hard to admit. In the end, it was because of his ego. Sure, helping the Amish boy get back had made Aaron feel a little selfless. But the truth was, Aaron loved solving the mystery of the cavern and teaching Jake and the Amish boy about it. It made him feel smart, important, and in control.

Now he was alone, broken, and not the least bit in control. Suddenly his heart ached for his family. He had many arguments with his brothers and parents, and afterward went to his room and spent hours thinking only about himself. Just thinking about that made him feel awful. He had worked hard to get away, to show them he was grown up, and able to do things independently. Now all he wanted was to be back with them. He hated to admit it, but sometimes his little brothers had embarrassed him. There were times he did not even want to be seen in public with them. Missing them as he was, he even longed for one of their Sunday Fundays.

Usually Aaron hated these family outings. It seemed as if each one started out the same, with his dad knocking on his door.

"C'mon Aaron, let's go. It's Sunday Funday," his dad always said. "Get your shoes on. We're heading out!"

Aaron groaned. "Are you kidding, Dad? I don't want to go. I hate going hiking. I want to work on my invention."

"Nope. It's Sunday and we do things as a family. And like it or not you are part of the family."

"But I don't want to go!" he yelled through the door, not bothering to open it. "You guys always want to hike somewhere that I hate. It's not fair that I have to go. Can't you leave me at home?"

Though he could not see him, Aaron had heard his dad's sigh from the hallway. "Aaron, we've been through this. There are six people in this family and we all enjoy different things. Some Sundays we are going to do what you want to do, and other times we are going to do what the other kids, or your mother and I, want to do."

Aaron pulled on a sweatshirt and, bypassing the socks, slipped on his tennis shoes. He opened the door and walked by his dad in silence, making his was downstairs. His mom was testing the baby-backpack carrier. She had already put Nathan in it, strapped him in, and placed him behind her. She hopped around to make sure the straps were tight so that he would not fall out. Nathan giggled with each bounce, then he grabbed a fistful of her hair, pulling tightly.

"I just don't get it," Aaron complained. "Why can't the family members who want to do the activity go, and those who don't can just stay home. I'm not going to enjoy myself, and that will probably ruin it for the rest of you."

Aaron had struck a nerve and his dad's face tightened. He had overheard his parents talking about this scenario in the kitchen earlier that morning. While he could not hear it all, Aaron knew his mom had pushed the "we do things as a family and he needs to learn" argument. Although what he needed to learn, Aaron was not sure about.

"Aaron, these things are important to us. Even if you don't enjoy them, you should appreciate that we do and be supportive, because we are a family. Your brothers don't like everything you do, yet they come along to activities you pick and they find ways to enjoy themselves. It's all about learning to put others before yourself."

Aaron's face flushed as the memory faded. He felt awful and could not believe how selfish he had been. The same could be said about doing his chores and helping around the house. It seemed like he was always arguing, it would have been easier, and frankly taken less time, just to do what was asked of him.

Then he thought about Jake. Although she did not have any siblings to contend with, she had a ton of responsibility and work to do around the house. And she always did it willingly. At first, he figured she was not as smart as he was, or maybe not as good at arguing her way out of stuff. At one time he thought she might even enjoy chores, but when he had asked her about it she had said, "No way. I don't think anyone *likes* doing chores. But I see how much work my dad does—waking before dawn, working the fields, repairing the equipment, fixing the house. And my mom doesn't get a lick of help around the house from him because my dad is so busy. They both work really hard. Have you ever taken the time to see what your parents do every day? How they spend their time? I'm sure they'd love to sit around. Who wouldn't? I just think it's only fair for me to pitch in."

Her words made more sense to him now. He had taken a lot of things for granted. When he got back, *if* he got back, he would try harder to be more helpful and to think of others—

A resounding crash echoed through the barn. Someone was there. *Must be my Amish buddy. Good! I'm anxious to start making the gears.* Aaron was about to call out, when he caught sight of who had entered. It was not his friend! Quickly, he sunk back and hid himself as best he could. A muscled Amish teenager walked in his direction. Had he been seen? He did not think so. Aaron recognized the face as soon as it came out of the shadows—Samuel.

Pausing, Samuel scanned the room. *He's looking for something*, Aaron thought. In the stall next to where he was hiding, a horse nickered. Samuel stared at the horse, then continued his search. Aaron followed his gaze.

The workbench!

Samuel covered the distance in only a few strides. He collected the remnants of the flashlight and placed them in a leather satchel draped over his shoulder. As he turned to leave, he spied the pile of broken gears. Hastily, he added them to the bag. When he reached the door,

STOLEN!

Samuel leaned forward and glanced out the barn's entrance like a thief on watch.

Aaron froze. What should he do? Without the broken gears, they would not be able to make replacements. And without new parts for the tree, they would not be able to open it. And if they could not open the tree…he did not want to even think about that. *I've got to stop him.*

"No!!" Aaron yelled.

Samuel jumped and peered into the barn's shadows. Aaron locked eyes with him but Samuel's initial look of fright turned from shock to mockery as he noticed Aaron's cast. He sneered, wrinkling his forehead, and then nodded with a grunt of satisfaction.

"Aaron?" It was the Amish boy. He was coming and just in time! Samuel's face turned dark. *Ha!* Aaron thought. *Caught!* It was Aaron's turn to gloat.

"In here! Quick! Samuel's here!"

Aaron lunged forward as best he could, intent on grabbing Samuel's legs. But the older boy was too fast and escaped Aaron's grasp, pushing him aside. The ground raced to meet him and Aaron collided hard into the packed dirt, his head ringing. Before everything faded to black, he saw Samuel's and the Amish boy's silhouettes in the doorway. For a moment Aaron thought they had him, but Samuel was larger and stronger. His friend was unprepared for the charging bull and Samuel escaped into the night.

Chapter 27
JAKE'S FUTURE

Not knowing what else to do, Jake continued walking to Aaron's house. What had happened? Where was the barn? Did Aaron's family even live there anymore? Carefully she approached, watching for any movement from the direction of the house. She kicked the dirt that had once been the barn's floor. Sadness clutched her heart as she remembered their first climb up the rickety old ladder that led to the loft. Aaron had been afraid. She could tell. He never would have admitted it, but she had seen the look of surprise in his eyes at how quickly she had climbed with no concern about the height or the missing loft boards. The truth was that she had been a little scared. But she wanted to make a good impression. She wanted to prove she was not a girly girl and could take care of herself.

There had been the chest with its gears. At that time, they had no idea what they were for. Now, they were the key to getting her home. For a moment, she wondered if she had overshot—maybe it was much further in the future than four years!

Moving on autopilot, she made her way to the large tree where they had found the buried diary and helium bottles. *Maybe we buried the chest and gears here?* Jake recalled the map the Amish boy had left them in the beautifully carved wooden box. She saw the words and directions as if they had been imprinted on her brain. After counting off the steps, she checked her position relative to the tree. She dropped to the ground and started to dig.

Her fingernails soon compacted with black dirt. After making slow progress, she cupped her hands and used them like a shovel. After a minute or two she stopped.

This isn't working, she thought. *I need a shovel.* She automatically turned toward the barn forgetting for a moment it was no longer there. *Darn it!*

Suddenly she heard voices behind her and quickly scrambled behind the tree. A sharp piece of the thick bark dug into her back and she stifled a yelp. The voices were muffled by the wind—boys' voices. She could not understand what they were saying.

Car doors opened and there were more voices. Jake peeked around the tree.

Near the house, the boys got into a van. At first, she did not recognize them. But as the last boy climbed in, he turned in her direction. She jerked her head back and was fairly certain he had not seen her. But she had seen him. Much taller than before, and growing into his larger frame, Jake recognized Aaron.

She could hardly believe how he had changed. His hair was thick and long now. In her time, it was a buzz cut, compliments of his dad's bathroom barber shop. Aaron's dad wore the same style, keeping it closely cropped. Aaron had told Jake that it was his dad's way of dealing with his receding hairline on his own terms. "I don't know why I have to suffer the same fate," Aaron had said. "I'm not the one losing my hair!" Jake had laughed, swirling her hand around the top of his head with a double pat as if he were a dog. She knew he hated when she did that, which was one of the reasons she did it.

Four years. She couldn't believe how long his hair was now. Not just longer, but blonder and put together, not styled but not haphazard either. His clothing was different too. In her time, Aaron put on whatever clothes he saw first—usually a tee shirt and running pants. He had complained that jeans just were not comfortable. She never understood, but he had said they felt funny. Today, he wore shorts and a patterned tee shirt covered by a casual, neutral-colored, button-down shirt. This was clearly a fashion statement!

As the van drove off, Jake crept carefully to the garage. Peering through the side window she saw the building was empty.

Good, no one home, she thought. *Maybe there is a shovel in there.*

She glanced to the rafters remembering the helium balloons Aaron had hidden there. Now it was bare except for a few long wooden planks. Under the rafters was a small pulley system used to suspend bikes in the winter months. Otherwise, the garage was bare—no storage bins, or toys, and most importantly no gardening tools such as a shovel!

Now what?

Jake exited the garage and noticed only a screen door barred the entrance to the house. She hesitated, maybe someone was home. Then again, perhaps they were on a quick errand and had plans to come right back.

I'll go in for just a minute, she thought. *I need to check a newspaper or calendar to see exactly how far in the future I am.*

Jake tiptoed on the wooden porch steps and squeezed the screen door's handle.

"Hello?" she yelled, pulling open the door. "Anybody here?"

No answer.

The front entry had been updated. A muted tan-colored paint replaced what had been aging wallpaper in her time. Jake smiled. She loved this house—the old hardwood floors, the classic yet simple wooden staircase, it even smelled the way she remembered. Aaron's mom loved to cook with heavy spices. Over the years, the smells must have permeated into the fabric, rugs, and draperies—subtle but still recognizable.

Walking into the family room, she stopped to inspect the family pictures lining the fireplace mantle. She picked one, admiring the panoramic view of an enchanting crystal blue lake at the foot of a majestic mountain; Aaron and family stood in the foreground, outfitted in hiking gear.

Colorado, Jake thought. Aaron had said that his family had always talked about going there someday. Jake was amazed how much bigger the boys were in the photo—how much had changed in just a few years. She had missed a lot. What if she could not get back? Replacing the picture, a feeling of nostalgia came over her.

With a deep sigh, she gazed past the footstool and made her way through the dining room and into the kitchen. Jake froze when she was startled by a loud click followed by the sound of rushing water. A moment later, she realized it was only the dishwasher cycling. Jake closed her eyes, slowly shaking her head.

The kitchen was clean. Aaron's mom was a stickler for keeping the place tidy even with four boys. Unfortunately for Jake, it meant that the recycling bin was empty so no newspapers were around for her to check the date. She made her way over to the small desk near the pantry and looked at a calendar. Someone had been adding activities, appointments, and birthdays to it. Jake checked the year—2010—it had worked! She was four years in the future. Satisfied, she decided that since she was already inside, she would explore a bit more before continuing her search for a shovel.

Knowing the house was empty, she bounded up the steps to Aaron's room. His furniture had been rearranged, and the room was painted with horizontal blue and green striped sections near the ceiling. He had a laptop computer now. It sat prominently in the center of the desk in sleep mode. The screen was dark, but lights indicated it had power. She hit the power button and a wavy purple screen saver danced across the screen.

Papers, discarded candy wrappers, pencils, and old video game cartridges littered the desktop. She wondered how he knew where anything was. Clicking the mouse, she tried to access his computer. A dialogue screen appeared requesting a password. Jake wrinkled her brow trying to get inside his mind. What would he use as a password? The first thing that came to mind was "helium." After all, it had been the key to getting into the tree. Typing in the letters, she hit enter.

Nothing.

After that, she tried everything she could think of—tree, barn, Amish, time travel, but nothing worked.

She gave up. She was wasting time.

When she was reaching to hit the power button again, to put the computer back in sleep mode, a precariously-stacked pile of papers fell off the desk. *Darn it.*

She gathered the items, wondering how the heck she would ever get them positioned the way they had been. Aaron might notice a difference, although considering his other messes she hoped he would never know. As she straightened the pile, a picture slipped out. She was about to replace it when she noticed it was a picture of Aaron and a girl, sitting on his front porch. It must have been recently taken because Aaron had the same hairstyle she had seen outside. He and the girl were smiling as if they had recently been laughing about something. Jake could not help but wonder who the girl was and was surprised that seeing her made Jake feel a little angry. She could tell by the look in Aaron's eyes that he liked her. The girl was cute with her hair in a ponytail and freckles...

"Oh my gosh!"

She looked closer and touched the picture. She knew who it was. Things had changed not only for Aaron, but her as well. Looking at the image Jake was shock to see her future self!

At the computer, Jake thought again about the password prompt. She could feel the blood pulsing through her veins as she pushed each key: J...A...K...E. Her finger hovered over the enter key. What if it worked? What did it mean?

She resisted. Knowing too much about the future was probably as bad as knowing too much about the past. Though she was insanely curious, she deleted the letters and pressed the button, returning the computer to its default state. She stood and looked out the window at the garden behind the house.

"The garden! That's it! There has to be a shovel there."

Turning to leave, she took one last look around the room and saw a large robot standing in the corner.

He finished it.

Her mind wandered back to their first meeting at the surplus store. Man, Aaron had been annoying back then. All she had wanted was to be friends, but he either made fun of everything she said, or ignored her completely. The whole project started with one small robot arm and its motors, pulleys, and gears...

Gears!

She smiled. She would not need a shovel after all.

Chapter 28
TWINKLE TWINKLE LITTLE STAR

W e've got to get them back!" Aaron yelled.
"Not so loud," the boy scolded, helping Aaron up.

Aaron winced and nodded in agreement. *Man,* he thought. *I am getting the snot kicked out of me.* The emotions, the loneliness, the uncertainty, and the pain—tears welled in the corner of his eyes, and Aaron fought hard to keep them in. Taking a deep breath, he held his composure together.

The boy squeezed his shoulder. "It will be okay. You'll be fine, and I will get you home."

Again the irony hit Aaron. How could a one hundred-year-old Amish kid know anything about something as complicated as the time cavern? How could he be so confident? Especially now that their only hope had been stolen. But the boy simply stared back with an angelic smile. Maybe it was time to go with the flow and stop being the control freak with all the answers. Maybe he should just trust the boy.

"Okay," he agreed. "But how will we ever get them back?"

"We don't need them. I already have everything we need."

"How?" Aaron started, "I have no idea how to get into that tree without the gears."

"I'm going to do as you suggested—we'll make new ones."

Aaron sighed in exasperation. Of course they needed to make new ones—duh. "How can we make anything without the old ones? We've got to find some way to get them back. I can't—"

Is that a smirk? What the heck, Aaron thought as he watched the boy's mouth curl upward. *He's smirking at me. I'm totally stuck here!*

"Is something funny?"

"I am sorry, Aaron," the boy said. "It's just that you are much different now. You used to be the one who had all the answers. Now you must trust me. It doesn't matter that Samuel has the gears."

Aaron watched as the boy produced an item from a satchel.

The diary.

"It's all here." The boy opened the pages, turning them as if he were handling a church missal. He tilted his head back like a librarian peering through the bottom half of her bifocals. "Look." The boy held up the book for Aaron to see.

For a moment, Aaron felt transported back to the tanning salon. The map to the tree now included the additional information that had been missing only the day before—details of the inner mechanism, pages of drawings with measurements of the different gears and parts they had collected. How was that possible?

"You were asleep," the boy explained as if he had read Aaron's mind. "But the excitement of the adventure kept me awake. I tried reciting a few of my favorite prayers, which usually helps when my mind is too active. But that was no good. I wanted to know how the pieces we found would fit together." The boy crossed to the empty bench. "Occasionally, I hear someone walking around in our house late at night. My father told me that when he can't sleep, he distracts his mind by reading."

Aaron could relate to that. Frequently, his thoughts kept him awake. Sometimes it was about school, but a lot of times it had been because of the tree. The best solution he found was to keep a small notebook near his bed so he could jot down notes about whatever he was thinking. This almost always helped. It was as if his thoughts were transported out of his mind and on to the page.

"So," the boy continued. "I got out of bed, came here, and studied each item. I took measurements and drew pictures of them. I also drew what I could remember from the tree."

Aaron did not know if the drawing of the interconnected gears was correct, but he knew immediately that these were the same drawings from the diary he had seen in the future. "Shall we get started?" The boy said, retrieving the diary from Aaron.

"Sure," Aaron replied, lost in thought.

"Wonderful," the boy said with an excited grin. "There are many pieces that I'll need your help with."

Pinewood derby cars were Cub Scout staples. Aaron had tolerated scouting most of the time, but the annual car race was something he always looked forward to. His dad helped him with the power tools. They used a jig saw to make the big cuts, and used a file, rasp, and sandpaper to finish the job. Aaron's other experience with tools had been when he helped his dad complete a room in their basement. He had gotten the chance to use a power saw and power drill during that project. For the most part, other than occasionally using a screwdriver, pretty much all of Aaron's experience with tools had been with ones that required being plugged into a wall socket. Most of these tools did not even exist this early in the century, and even if they had, the Amish would never have used them. As a result helping the Amish boy make the intricate gears proved to be a challenge.

At first, he thought the boy had been joking when he handed Aaron a board and a rectangular wood block with a handle on top.

"Plane this please," the boy requested. "It has to be exactly one inch thick. It's a good thing the gears are all the same thickness."

Turning over the wood block, Aaron discovered a metal blade sticking out below the smooth surface of the tool. "Hmm," he mumbled. "I'm not exactly sure what to do with this."

"Here," the boy said as he took the tool and placed it on the board. "You need to run the side with the blade along the board. It will shave off sections that stick out and make the board very flat." Gripping the tool with two hands, one on the handle and one on the back of the block, the Amish boy swept across half the board in one smooth motion. "See?"

Thin strips of curled wood rolled off the blade on the underside of the tool. They reminded Aaron of birthday present ribbons.

"Make sure you plane it to one inch."

Aaron took the plane and measuring stick the boy handed him. It took a couple of tries to get the hang of it, but soon Aaron got into a groove. Every few swipes he measured and then turned the board over and planed the other side. Just as his arm was starting to tire, he finished and handed it to the boy.

The boy inspected the board by running his hand across both sides. "Good. I'll get to work cutting out the different pieces." He handed Aaron another piece of wood. "Same thickness please."

Aaron's eyes grew wide, and he rubbed his aching arm. "You need more?"

"Yes," the boy replied without missing a beat. "This one, plus one more, will probably be enough."

Aaron sighed. "I'm going to need a little break," he admitted ashamed. "If it's okay, I'd like to watch what you do for a moment to see what comes next."

"Certainly," the boy replied, motioning for Aaron to join him at the workbench. "Come on over."

The boy took out a metal V-shaped tool and after referring to his notes, adjusted the angle and locked it into place by turning a screw at the top. Aaron noticed that one leg could draw marks and the other had a sharp point that the boy stuck in the middle of the board. He rotated it around, making a perfect circle.

A compass, Aaron thought. He had used one in art class but did not understand what use they could have in the real world. Now he knew. Taking a small, oddly-shaped saw, the boy carefully cut the board by following the line of the circle. He did a good job, but clearly the result was not perfect. The boy then drew notches along the perimeter of the circle as described in his notes.

The boy unrolled a piece of leather—inside of it, little pockets held five or six tools. At first Aaron thought that they were screwdrivers but as each was removed, he noticed the ends were wider and sharper.

"This is a set of chisels," he explained. "We'll use them to cut the notches in the gears."

With deliberate motions, the boy showed him how to use a hammer and chisel to finish the gear cuts. Aaron took over this job while the Amish boy planed the other boards. Aaron was thankful for the reprieve, and also happy his friend had not asked if he wanted to switch. He would have been embarrassed, but he would have also agreed.

As he worked, the boy began to whistle.

"Hey," Aaron said. "Maybe we could listen to some music to help pass the time."

"What do you mean?"

"You know, turn on a radio…" Then he remembered. It was too early for *radios*.

"A what?"

"Never mind. I forgot. It hasn't been invented yet."

"What hasn't?"

"Well there is this thing in my time called a radio. It is basically a box with knobs. When you turn it on, music comes out. The knob changes stations for different types of music."

"You're not serious, right?" The boy laughed. "How could that be possible? There would not be enough room in such a box."

"The music doesn't come from the box. It comes from a radio station." Aaron realized it would be nearly impossible to explain about radio stations and even if he did, the boy would never believe him. It was hard to believe how much he took for granted. He hardly even listened to the radio anymore, except in the car when his mom had it on. Usually he used his iPod. Imagine if he had brought that along! The Amish boy would have freaked! Hundreds of songs in something small enough to hold in one hand. It can even play games and show movies…movies…ha! What he would pay to see the look on his friends face after showing him one of those.

"Maybe we could sing a song?" Aaron suggested.

"Okay." The boy nodded and started to sing:

In der Stillen Einsamkeit,
Findest du mein lob bereit
Grosser Gott Erhöre mich,
Denn mein Herze suche dich.

"No way!" Aaron interrupted.

"What?"

"That's Twinkle Twinkle Little Star!"

The boy wrinkled his forehead.

"That song you are singing," Aaron explained. "The melody. That is a song we sing. It's called Twinkle Twinkle Little Star." Aaron sang the first few lines. "Maybe we got our song from yours."

"I do not think that could be," the boy countered. "What you sang is not what our song is about. *In der Stillen Einsamkeit,* means "In the Still Isolation." It's about God always being there, through every season. The song says that God is never still, though he may be silent. The song says my praise is always there and my heart will always seek him."

The boy taught Aaron the words. It was odd at first to sing in a different language, but in some ways it made the song more powerful than the silly words from his time.

Afterward, the Amish boy asked Aaron to teach him a song and although Aaron was too old to be singing it, he thought of *Row, Row, Row, Your Boat* because it would be easy to teach, and frankly, singing it together would be fun. After singing it in unison the first few times, Aaron started a round one stanza later. The two kept it going for quite some time, until they laughed so hard they could not keep the melody going.

The day continued in much the same way and Aaron lost track of time until he noticed the sunlight that had been streaming into the barn had started casting long shadows. He also realized he was hungry. As if on cue, the Amish boy left and returned with another strange meal. Aaron decided not to ask what it was, fearing the details would turn his stomach. And what did it matter—it tasted good!

By nightfall, they had cut all the parts and most had been sanded to make them as accurate as possible. They connected the gears by placing them on wooden dowels and tested the interlocking teeth. Aaron thought back to the day he and his brothers had spent building things out of tinker toys. They had spent hours making different contraptions. It was one of the few times he could remember having such a good time with them. There had been no arguments—just fun.

"That's it," the boy said, cleaning the tools and slapping dust off his hands.

"Tomorrow—we can go back!"

Chapter 29

FOUR YEARS BACK

Jake stepped back and admired her work. Everything was in place. Looking at the complex set of gears, she marveled at how intricately they fit with the original mechanism in the tree. Part of her wondered how it had happened. The original pieces could not have been made from wood. Why were these?

The robot had been the key to her discovery.

As soon as she had seen it, she knew Aaron had hidden the parts inside. Ingenious. They had been integrated so that they looked functional but they were easily removed. When you knew what to look for, they stood out like a sore thumb, as they were the only things made of wood in the entire design.

Finding the parts was not the big issue. Determining what to do with them had been the problem. Sure, she would eventually figure out how to put them in their proper places inside the tree. But she had no way to return them. If her plan worked, she would go back four years. That would leave the parts inside the tree and missing from the robot.

Aaron would eventually find the missing parts, but how could the mystery be explained? She thought about leaving a note in the robot but did not know what to say.

"Aaron, it's me, Jake. I took the parts to get back to my own time four years ago. They are in the tree."

or

"Part's in the tree."

or

"What happened to the barn?"

The truth of the matter was she wondered what the future held for them. Why was the barn gone? And what about that picture? Of course, it did not make sense to leave a note. If she did not get back then none of this would be real, and if she did, the "future Jake" would already know that she had taken them. In fact, it occurred to her that her future self already knew all this stuff, but chose not to guide her. Argh! It was all so confusing and strange!

In the end she took the parts without leaving any note. Aaron would figure it out, and if not, her future self would explain. At least that was what she hoped.

After opening the tree, Jake made the trek down the curved path to what she and Aaron now called "the helium room." How different this was compared to her first journey inside the organic blue luminous passageway. She had been afraid, uncertain, and filled with dread. Now she strode confidently.

Reaching into her pack, she pulled out one of the helium canisters. Goosebumps formed on her skin and she shuddered when she realized how fortunate it had been that she brought them along.

Inside the cavern, she found the old familiar bucket next to the control levers. In her own time, she had figured out how to keep the cavern vortex open indefinitely by using water from the stream. After four years, she would have thought that she and Aaron would have rigged a more permanent solution than her hose system. Knowing

Aaron as she did, she half expected to find a network of pipes, complete with some kind of perpetual pump—after all, he had finished the robot. Yet, here the cavern was. Basically the same as they had found it, except for the location of the bucket.

On second thought, she realized the only time it was necessary to keep the vortex open was when using the moon setting. Any other setting immediately transported the person, and there was no need to keep the vortex open.

For this trip, there was no need for the moon setting. Jake filled the bucket from the pool and ran back up the steep path toward the controls. Nearing the top, her pace slowed and she stopped to catch her breath.

Easy Jake.

She carefully poured the water into the receiving tube.

Here we go again!

With the main lever engaged, the tunnel door closed, the vents came to life, and starry images danced on the dome. Although she did not understand why it worked, the familiarity of knowing how to operate the levers was comforting. The inverted cavern inside the moon setting was almost a mirror image of this one, with a few bizarre differences that she still did not understand. What was with the multiple pathways leading to the edge of the cavern? How had she become trapped inside? These were mysteries that she would have to solve some other time. For now it was time to go home!

One thing she liked better in the other cavern was the control panel. Adjusting to the right star was much easier there. Here, she struggled with the levers to find Proxima Centauri, but finally locked it in.

She slung her pack over her shoulder. Only a couple of minutes were left before the water ran out and the vortex closed. Walking along the invisible bridge Jake felt different as she neared the time field. Unlike when using the moon setting, the cavern vibrated more violently this time. The air pulsed as reality fragmented and distortions emanated out from the center. A memory flashed and she recalled the last time she had seen Aaron. She remembered sensing his reluctance to enter the vortex.

Was something wrong? Perhaps the vortex was not supposed to work this way. The stars were aligned exactly as they should be. The target was Proxima Centauri. She was sure of that. Using it should take her back four years. This was the only choice if she wanted to get back to her own time. After all, what was the worst that could happen?

Closing her eyes tightly, she stepped forward.

Jake braced herself and entered the vortex. Neither of her other two trips had been anything like this. Entering the time field she felt an uncomfortable sensation—a thought that her foot would never land on solid ground overwhelmed her. It was like expecting another step when you had already reached the top of the stairs. At least, that was how the sensation had started. Jake saw her foot elongate and little by little her body disintegrated until only a small thread held her to the bits and pieces that had left. Somehow her body was gone, but her mind was still there, connected by a very thin and tenuous link. Suddenly the pieces were thrust back together again. She opened her eyes, and at first saw nothing—white blindness. Then images resembling a watercolor painting that had being washed out by a strong rain started to appear. She was not sure if what she was seeing was real, but as her eyesight normalized, she also regained her other senses. Bird songs and the smell of wildflowers brought her home, or what she hoped was home.

While reality rebuilt itself, she wondered how she would appear to anyone walking through the forest. Would she simply appear out of thin air? And what about the ants, flies, and other things that had occupied the space she entered? Where did they go?

Jake rushed to the tree and came upon the hose—just as she had left it. Elation filled her, and she breathed deeply.

She raced to the creek, following the path of the hose and found the rest of it curled neatly on the creek's bank. It was arranged too perfectly to have gotten that way by accident.

How is this possible?

She scanned the stream, the fields, and looked around the forest. Not only had someone moved the hose, but they had left it for her to find. Whoever it was had trapped her inside the moon setting.

Who did this to me?!

Chapter 30

SHODDING

Come along Sarah." Samuel slowed so his sister could keep up. He had put off the chore long enough. Their horse needed to be shod and he had promised Sarah he would let her watch.

"But why must I carry everything?" she asked while struggling to carry the wooden box.

"Because, it is the only way you can help. I will be doing all the real work, so the least you can do is carry the tools." Samuel was particularly proud of his shodding toolbox. He had made it from a simple rectangular design—nothing very special—but the large eyehook handle in the center made it easy to carry, and he had placed the tool notches along the edges, making it perfectly balanced. Well, when carried correctly. He thought of helping Sarah as she continued, her arms wrapped around the entire box while she tried to hug it to her chest. They had only a few more steps to reach the waiting horse, tied to a fence. off to the right, the barn loomed. What he really wanted to do was inspect the objects he had stolen the day before.

That boy and Sarah's friend were in trouble. He wondered exactly who that boy was. Where had he come from? Samuel had not seen him around the community or at Sunday services. The few times he heard him talk, his speech was unusual. Not so much an accent, but his words—many of them Samuel had never heard before.

"Now what?" Sarah asked.

Samuel realized he had not been paying attention. "Take a seat and watch. I'll explain."

Sarah hopped on a hay bale, picked a piece of straw, and stuck it between her teeth. Samuel pulled the toolbox toward him and calmed the horse. Truth be told, he enjoyed doing this. Horses gave him a serene feeling that he rarely felt otherwise. Years earlier his father had taken him to watch and learn from the Amish farrier. Samuel had been fascinated and returned often. Eventually he became an apprentice.

Taking a pair of pincers, Samuel held them out for Sarah to see. "I use this tool to remove the shoe," he explained. After pulling out the nails, he positioned the horse's foot for her to see. "Notice the hoof part here? It is similar to our finger nails except much bigger and thicker. As strange as it might seem, the horse walks around on its toenails."

"Interesting," Sarah said. "But why does a horse need shoes? Wild horses don't need them?"

"A wild horse runs every day and that wears down their nails naturally. Our horses do not have that chance while working for us on the farm or pulling the carriage. They are used for specific purposes, and their nails will grow and even crack if they are not trimmed and protected with shoes."

Samuel showed her how to trim the horse's hoof and pointed to a place on its sole which he called the "frog," which made Sarah laugh. He described how proper trimming ensured the horse stayed balanced, otherwise, the horse could damage its legs.

After the hoof was properly prepared, Samuel straightened the shoe and checked to make sure it fit correctly. Then he nailed it back into place.

"See how the nail is sticking out from the top of the hoof? I need to cut part of that excess off and then use these tongs, called clinchers, to pull the remaining nail against the hoof. Then I'll hammer the nail, bending it down in place so that it holds the shoe and won't get caught on anything." Samuel rummaged through the tool box, searching for a hammer. When he did not find one he said, "Sarah, go to the barn and find a hammer. There should be one near the other tools."

As Sarah walked, she smiled—happily. Samuel was being nice, answering her questions, and genuinely interested in teaching her. Maybe things would return to normal.

Entering the barn, she spied the hammer and skipped toward it. A stream of sunlight caught her eye when it reflected off something inside a wood-slat box. Whatever it was, it had been covered haphazardly. Sarah brushed aside the cloth and stared in disbelief. This could not be. How was it possible? How did these get here?

Without a second thought, she ran out of the barn.

"Sarah!" Samuel yelled. He had been holding up the horse's foot for some time and he was getting a cramp.

What is taking her so long?

"Sarah, where are you?"

With a grunt, he released the horse, kicked the toolbox aside, and strode to the barn.

"Sarah, how hard can it be to find a hammer?" He looked around and noticed she was nowhere in sight.

Where did she go?

Then he saw that his box was uncovered. She must have been involved with whatever those two boys were doing. Samuel knew exactly where she had gone.

Chapter 31
FOLLOWING AARON

Jake had licked the seal of the envelope and tasted the none-to-pleasant mixture of adhesive and paper.

Yuk!

The only thing worse would be if she got a paper cut while licking the envelope. She wrote in big block letters on the back.

FOR AARON'S EYES ONLY!

The exclamation point was a nice touch—kind of a warning sign implying "or else." Another exclamation point or underlining would have been overkill. *I don't want to draw too much attention to it.*

The letter inside was only a precaution—a backup in case her plan failed, which would be par for the course after recent events. She wondered if she was doing the right thing. Writing a note in the present did not seem nearly as dangerous as doing so in the past or the future. She was sure Aaron would not agree, he would say that it would not matter when in time something was written down. Passing information from one time to another could always be dangerous in his mind. As far as Jake was concerned, she felt the present would be the safest place to share as much information as you knew. And if she was wrong, well that was a risk she was willing to take. She was not sure her plan would work and if somehow Aaron made it back, and she did not, she wanted him to know where she had gone.

Following the beam of her flashlight, Jake stepped over a large branch that blocked the path. It was dark—really dark—a *no-moon-and-a-cloudy-sky-that-hid-the-starlight* kind of dark. Sneaking out of her house and going to the cavern at night had seemed like a good idea. But now she was not so sure. Not being able to see much more than the small area her flashlight illuminated made the journey feel really far.

She had to locate a place to hide the note where only Aaron would find it. The answer came to her quickly. Plus she needed to get some more canisters of helium for the return trip. Suddenly the path widened.

The barn! Finally.

Jake doused the light, concerned she might be spotted. The last thing she wanted was for one of Aaron's brothers to see her... or his parents. How could she possibly explain what she was doing? Holstering the flashlight in her back pocket, Jake entered the barn.

Geesh! It's even darker in here. She felt her way toward the ladder.

As she climbed each rung she gave them a little bounce, testing their strength. The hayloft was cool, and her skin pimpled with goosebumps. She sensed she was not alone. Crouching low, she listened. There was a scratching sound—no, not scratching—something moving perhaps? Then she heard a thumping and humming, and Jake twitched instinctively moving away from the sound.

C'mon Jake, turn on the light.

The night breeze shifted and the humming and thumping sound stopped. Jake let out a sigh just as something wet scratched her hand. She screamed and swatted it away. Grabbing the flashlight, she flicked it on.

Two eyes stared back at her.

"Calico!" she scolded. "You scared me half to death!"

She should have known. Ever since she and Aaron had found the stray cat wandering around the farm, Jake knew the mangy animal hunted for mice in the barn. Jake raced to the loft doors to check if anyone had heard her scream. After a few moments, when there was no movement from the house, she turned toward the old chest.

There it was. Almost exactly as they had found it. Emotion washed over her as she thought about how this had been where their adventures had begun. Then she felt sadness. Why was the barn gone in the future? What had happened to it?

"Hopefully, you'll never have to read this," she said, placing the note inside the chest and removing two helium canisters. Calico jumped on top, curled into a ball, and closed her eyes.

"Stay here and guard it my friend."

Jake squished the small yellow plug and rolled it between her fingers. Quickly, she jammed one in her ear, and repeated with another.

I don't know why we didn't think of this sooner.

While she had gotten accustomed to the loud, pounding, cavern vibrations there did not seem to be a reason for her to go deaf! She had spied the package of earplugs next to a set of screwdrivers before leaving the house and decided to bring them along at the last minute.

As she started the cavern, she nodded appreciatively at her foresight. Yup, much better! The vibrations pulsed through her bones, but it was much less annoying with the sound muffled.

Wait 'til I tell Aaron. I can imagine the look on his face saying, 'Why didn't I think of that!'

Jake set the cavern to the moon setting just in case Aaron was there. She waited for fifteen minutes, then decided there was no point to wait longer. Time to move on. Jake took hold of the levers and manipulated them into their new positions. The star field responded. Jake enjoyed the power of manipulating the universe. It was like playing a giant video game. Finally the red circle locked on target. She was going back one hundred years through time. She would follow Aaron, find out what had happened, and then bring him home!

Jake double-checked her backpack, mustered her courage, and once more marched to the shimmering waters below.

Chapter 32

CONFLUENCE!

S hoo!" Aaron said, waving his hands. But the rabbit remained. Having crept out from under a nearby bush, it had watched him for the last fifteen minutes. Amazing. It was one of the few animals Aaron had ever seen in the forest. He figured they had some sixth sense that told them to stay away—but not this one.

"Why isn't it afraid of us?" Aaron asked.

The Amish boy turned away from the gear he was working on. "Perhaps it doesn't think you could ever catch it with that leg of yours."

Was that a joke? Aaron thought.

The boy smiled.

It was a joke! Aaron burst out laughing, sending the rabbit scurrying off into the brush. The boys looked at one another then laughed even louder.

Aaron worked to perfect one of the gears they had made, cleaning out a notch with a rasp. He understood now how the wood gears in the future fit so perfectly into the mechanism. Making them just right was a meticulous process. Place the gears, fit them together, test them, take them out, sand them, adjust the notches, make minor tweaks, replace—then repeat. They had been working at it for hours after arriving at the tree early in the morning. Aaron had thought they would simply put them in, and off they would go. He could not have been more wrong. Even with the careful cutting, planing and all the skill and craftsmanship of the young Amish boy, they still found each piece needed at least minor, and some major, adjustments.

"Of course we will need to make modifications," the boy had explained. "Nothing works perfectly the first time." Now Aaron knew why the boy had packed his tools at the start of the day. Looking now at the leather satchel, Aaron thought about how this was his young friend's equivalent of the modern-day backpack.

Putting down the rasp, Aaron rubbed the ache in his forearm. Every muscle in his body was in pain, probably from his body compensating for his bum leg.

"Done?" the boy asked, noticing his pause.

"I think so. I say we try again."

"How many tries is this?" the boy asked.

"Not sure," Aaron replied. "I stopped keeping track after twelve." Aaron examined his hands. After hours of scraping, chipping, and sanding, the reward of his efforts was blisters—and a lot of them. They were little reminders of this adventure, painful, but in some ways rewarding as well.

As the boy loaded the gears, Aaron thought about the tree. How it was the center of everything. It had control over time and with that control, Aaron could go anywhere, change events, and alter history or the future. In many ways, it was all powerful. Strange how such a powerful thing would be in a tree. *Like the tree of knowledge,* Aaron thought.

"Are you going to look?" the boy asked, lending Aaron an outstretched hand.

"What?" Aaron asked. "Oh, nope." Instead, Aaron handed him the last gear and parked his philosophical thoughts. "I think I'll stay here—there's no point in getting up. You know what they say, 'fool me once, shame on me...fool me twice, shame on you.'"

"Shame me...what?"

Aaron shook his head dismissively, "It's a saying. Let me know if you need—" but he never finished. The low, booming sound of the tree's sidewall giving way sounded as the Amish boy turned the tree's crank.

"You're missing it!" he said as he let go and the crank's momentum completed the task.

"Just my luck," Aaron said, struggling to rise. He used the tree as leverage.

The Amish boy beamed with excitement. "Let's go!"

Sarah stomped through the forest, intent on finding the tree. Though she did not want to believe it, she knew how resourceful her friend could be. She needed to make sure. Halfway through the forest, she heard it—a loud echoing sound.

"No!" she cried and began to run toward the noise.

She was too late. As she neared the clearing, the boys entered the gaping maw in the tree. She dropped to her knees on the forest floor and covered her eyes with her hands. Tears formed and began to flow down her cheeks.

"Now what?" she asked aloud. "What am I to do?"

THE INVERTED CAVERN

～

"I can't believe I'm saying this," Aaron started, "but hand me the diary. I want to write some things down."

The Amish boy hesitated but then handed it over. Aaron remembered the boy's comments about how precious paper was.

"Tell you what," Aaron said, giving the diary back. "I'll capture the experiments in my notebook then you can copy the ones that work in the diary. I don't yet know why, but I think it is important we capture this in the diary."

"Because?"

"Well, mostly because I noticed how much we wrote in your version…" He paused and thought twice about sharing too much of what he knew was going to happen. "Let's just say I think having the information in more than one place would be a good idea."

Aaron placed his notebook on his backpack, using it as a makeshift desk. The Amish boy sat on the platform next to him, which overlooked the expansive cavern. He held his own nineteenth- century version—diary, quill, ink, and leather satchel. Aaron shrugged—some things change, but in many ways they stay the same—variations on a theme.

"How will we do these experiments?"

Aaron flipped back a couple of pages in his notebook. "Hey," the Amish boy said, pointing at a picture pasted on one of the papers. "That was from the book you showed me and your friend Jake in the future."

"Good memory," Aaron replied. "This is a list of the closest stars to earth. I thought we would start with these top ten and work our way to the moon setting. We can also try a few random stars first. Maybe there is a certain order we have to follow to make it work."

CONFLUENCE!

The boy hesitated.

"Is anything the matter?"

"Well I was thinking…" He tapped his quill nervously and turned to a drawing he had been working on. At the top of the page was a series of pictures showing the phases of the moon from a small crescent on the left side to the full moon in the center and ending with another crescent on the right side. The boy pointed to a blank space next to the final drawing.

"New moon," Aaron formed the words on his lips without actually speaking them. He thought back. After landing and breaking his leg, he did not remember much of anything other than the pain. But had there been a moon?

"What are you saying? Was there a new moon the night I arrived and we tried the cavern?"

The Amish boy nodded. "I've been thinking and realized that the new moon was something that was different from when I went into the vortex."

Aaron considered it. "Interesting. So you think that during a new moon that the moon setting doesn't work in the cavern?"

The boy nodded but did not meet Aaron's gaze.

"Why would that make a difference?" Aaron said more to himself than to the boy. "Even so, in the cavern the moon appears as a large full moon. In fact, I don't remember ever seeing different phases of the moon in the cavern."

The boy shrugged and Aaron felt bad. The Amish boy had a point that was worth exploring. He did not have a better theory.

"I like it!" Aaron added, slapping the boy on the shoulder. This would solve our problems if you're right. After all, the moon isn't new anymore. I say we fire up the cavern and give it a go!"

"Fire up?"

"Sorry, a figure of speech. Let's get the water and turn on the cavern. We've got work to do!"

Clutching the tree bark near the entrance, Sarah peered into the passageway. She brushed aside the sweat on her brow and took a step. The ground, if it was ground, was soft and spongy—like moss. The walls were the color of a cloudless, blue, midday sky. Here and there small roots protruded from the walls. It was alive, yet unnatural.

Feeling both hot and cold, Sarah fought the urge to run. She continued further down and the natural light from the forest diminished. The feeling of being swallowed down the gullet of a giant beast was overwhelming. The walls closed in around her until finally she entered a room.

The boys were not there, and she did not know where they had gone. Taking a step farther, Sarah discovered the answer—another passageway, but this one was different from the first. It appeared perfectly round and smooth. Turning her head to better position her ear, she made out the faint sound of voices. They had to be in there, but where was there? She heard the animated rise and fall of an argument. Another step and she stood directly in front of the tunnel. It was long, very long and perfectly straight.

More voices. Her friend was in trouble. She knew this would happen. There was no reason for him to come back here. After all the trouble she had gone through, she had not been able to stop what was happening. Part of her wanted to close her eyes and just run to them. But that was not smart. At the doorway to the long tunnel, she bowed her head, recited a silent prayer, and then reluctantly stepped in.

Confluence!

Samuel would not have believed it possible, but he had seen it with his own eyes. Like petrified prey, he stood in the forest frozen in place as he watched his younger sister walk *into* the tree. At the very pit of his stomach, in the core of his being, a primal warning screamed inside him. His own curiosity kept him mute. Well that and the fact that his sister did not appear surprised or even overly frightened, just a bit hesitant as she entered. He thought she must have been there before and knew the tree's secrets. There was no other explanation for her courage. But what was this tree? And more importantly, why was Sarah determined to enter into it? Something big, something important was happening. He had suspected that from the time she first came to him with a crazy story that she later recanted. Finding the magic lantern had confirmed his suspicions. He should have known for certain when it went missing. Sarah knew much more than he did, and it was time that he found out for himself. The answers, were in that tree.

Because of his bum leg, Aaron waited while the Amish boy retrieved the water. He felt guilty that he could not do more but the boy understood. Aaron looked down at the center of the pool where the action usually took place. The platform was high, like the upper deck of a major-league baseball field. From this distance, the tonal vents surrounding the pool could not be seen. They were completely covered by a substance similar to sand but more solid. Walking on the "shore" of the pool left no footprints.

The tube that transformed water into the semi-opaque drops

stretched into the center of the cavern without any stabilizing cables supporting it. It looked heavy and with the addition of the water and whatever magic happened inside, he wondered how it stayed suspended without bending. The cavern was an odd confluence of nature—the tree and water, with science—gears, vents, harmonics, the time vortex.

Although Aaron remained fascinated by the cavern, he was also homesick. He even missed his brothers who previously he had considered annoying. Of course he loved his mom and dad, but he had not realized just how much he enjoyed being around them. There had been arguments—quite a few actually. But that was mostly his fault. He did not like being wrong and when he was, he had a tendency to argue even more. Sometimes he was being stubborn, but mostly he argued in an attempt to prove he was not wrong.

"Ready?" The boy had made it back.

"Oh, yeah."

"What do you think about the new moon theory?" the boy asked breathlessly, setting the bucket on the platform. "Should we go straight to the moon setting and see what happens?"

Distracted by other thoughts, Aaron had forgotten about the boy's hypothesis. "I say we start with what we know works," he blurted. "Maybe the star that is the third furthest away. Let's have a few successes first. It won't take that much longer anyway."

"Why do you want to start there?"

"I don't know. At least if some settings work right off the bat, I'll feel better." Aaron thought he saw the boy shake his head in disagreement while he poured the water. But he said nothing.

"Do you want to pull the levers?" the boy asked.

"No, you are there, go ahead. While you do that, I'll grab the notebook and come on over."

As the boy pulled the main control lever, the start of the sequence began. Aaron's eyes followed the events as they cascaded throughout the cavern—the first drop fell, the pool started vibrating, the lights danced on the cavern's dome, and finally the tunnel leading to the helium room sealed. As the door closed, Aaron swore he heard something. It was hard to tell from where he was standing, but it sounded like a yelp. Not a scream, but more like someone calling out in surprise. He strained to listen but it had disappeared—the entrance fully sealed.

"Did you hear that?" he asked the boy.

"Hear what?"

"I don't know. Maybe it was nothing. But I thought I heard something come from the tunnel."

The boy stared past Aaron toward the cavern's entrance. "I didn't hear anything. What did it sound like?"

"I'm not certain. I thought it was a person."

Aaron heard the noise again. "There did you hear it that time?"

The boy shook his head slightly.

Fine, Aaron thought. *I probably just imagined it.*

Trapped. That word repeated over and over inside Samuel's head as he walked inside the tree. He and Michael had frequently caught stew rabbits by laying traps near the entrance to their warrens. Walking through the underground passage, Samuel felt a sudden connection with one of his prey. This was exactly what he thought a rabbit burrow would look like. Of course, the rabbits did not know they were walking into a trap.

But Sarah had entered—cautiously to be sure—and she was somewhere ahead. Even though she had kept secrets from him, she was still his sister, and it was his duty to help her. Circling down the winding passageway, he braced a hand against the wall and felt its dampness. As he pulled away, a slight bit of blue luminescence shown on his hand. Immediately he rubbed at it even as it started to fade.

Entering the larger chamber, Samuel breathed a short-lived sigh of relief until he saw another tunnel. There was no exit so Sarah must have gone in that direction. When he reached the entrance of the second tunnel, he saw Sarah's silhouette up ahead. He stepped in and picked up the pace so he would not fall too far behind.

Then the tunnel rumbled and darkened. At first Samuel thought Sarah had simply stumbled and was blocking the light, but then he understood what was actually happening. The tunnel was collapsing. Sarah screamed, but her terror was quickly muffled as the tube enveloped her. The walls continued to fall in reaching for him. Instinct told him to turn and run, but instead he raced forward to save his sister. He had only gone three steps when he tripped and fell flat. Samuel was quickly consumed. The pressure from the tunnel crushed his back, shoulders, thighs and head—cocooning him. It was a trap, and he was the rabbit.

Aaron closed his eyes in anticipation. What if this failed? What next? The familiar sounds of the cavern resonated throughout his body and rattled his bones. His broken leg was affected differently by the vibrations—some kind of tingling. Not a bad feeling just different.

"It works!" the boy cheered.

Aaron opened one eye a sliver. Sure enough, the swirling vortex sprouted, ushering in the time portal. Relief. This star setting worked. Aaron confirmed the targeted star Wolf 359. Aaron wondered what the deal was with that star, so many of the other ones had such cool names like Proxima Centauri, Sirius, and Epsilon Eridani. Were there three hundred and fifty-eight other stars named Wolf before this one?

"Should we try the next one?" the boy asked anxiously.

"Yeah, sure."

Before moving on, the boy drew a picture in his diary showing the lever positions and the words:

YEARS BACK - 7.8

"What are you doing?" Aaron asked.

"I want to capture the control lever locations for each star with its corresponding time jump in case we need them in the future."

"Tell you what," Aaron offered. "I'll capture the information and you can focus on working the levers. That way it'll go faster."

Aaron copied the next star on the list underlining the name— *Barnard's Star.* "As if Wolf 359 was not weird enough," he mumbled.

It turned out that Barnard's star worked just as well as Wolf 359, as did the rest of the stars close to earth. Aaron finished the notations in the diary and handed it back. The Amish boy checked them over and added a few comments with his quill. It was like being graded by a teacher.

When he had finished, the boy asked excitedly, "Is it time?"

It was time. The rest of these tests were meaningless if he could not get the moon setting to work. No future. No going home. Only backward. The "new moon" theory was interesting, but was that why the cavern had not worked? There was one way to find out.

"Okay, let's do it."

The cavern brightened as the radiance of the full moon rose above the horizon. Aaron watched the boy's gaze fixate skyward. The levers shadows' lengthened as the moon climbed higher in the cavern.

"Here comes the lock!"

The stars, the moon, the shadows—everything froze. The boys' heads fell in unison to stare at the pool.

They waited.

No vortex.

No portal.

The boy's shoulders slumped. "I thought it would work," he said, sounding betrayed.

"Why would everything else work?" Aaron yelled, throwing his notebook. "Let's go take a look. Maybe we're missing something."

When they reached the water's edge, Aaron pinched the bridge of his nose to stave off a headache. Even though the vortex had not appeared, the cavern vents were as loud as ever. Shouting over the noise, Aaron signaled to the pool with a nod. "Let's both go take a look."

The Amish boy nodded. Walking on the invisible submerged bridge had always been a challenge, but doing so with the addition of a crutch and one Amish boy made it precarious.

Halfway to the center, it happened.

Aaron had been concentrating on the spot where the opaque droplets fell into the pool. This was where the vortex should have been. But suddenly Aaron's crutch missed the bridge while he was in mid-step. There was no way to recover. Aaron pitched forward, the world spun, and he pivoted as a mishmash of images: water, crutch, stars, platform, moon rushed by. A feeling of light headedness washed over him.

Earlier that year, Sarah had hiked with her friends to a nearby lake to go swimming. She was not good at it and hated to go. Even though her undergarments were not revealing, taking off clothes in front of her friends embarrassed her, and she had never felt comfortable in the water.

The lake water was so clear that they could see the minnows swimming between their legs. This had given Sarah's "friend" Mary the idea of playing an underwater racing game. But Sarah knew that Mary just wanted to show off. She was the best swimmer and could keep her eyes open under water. Nonetheless, Mary convinced the others to go along with the idea of tossing a large metal soup ladle in the water for them to fetch. After some discussion, they had decided to take turns to find the object instead of racing all at once.

Mary had gone first. She stood facing the shore, while the other girls stayed in the shallow water facing her.

"Mary, close your eyes!" Anne had said, drawing back her arm to throw the ladle. Everyone counted down: "One, two, three—throw!"

After another count to five, to allow the ladle to sink, Mary had taken a deep breath and set off. Sarah had seen exactly where the ladle and been thrown, but she had still been surprised by how quickly Mary had found it, completing the task with only one breath.

No one would beat her time.

They each took their turns and when Sarah's time came, she had wished she were home. She hated the game. Closing her eyes, she had heard them count. It was Mary's turn to throw the ladle. For some reason Mary had a habit of teasing Sarah, though she did not know why. The girls yelled *"Throw!"* and Sarah heard the ladle splash far behind and to her right. The girls gasped and one admonished, "Mary!" Sarah figured it was because she had thrown the ladle a long way, making the challenge even greater.

Sarah had been angry. Why did Mary have to do that? Why did she always try to make Sarah look weak? Well, she had been determined to show her—show them all. Her anger fueled her desire to prove herself and gave her courage. After the count to five, Sarah opened her eyes, stared at the girls, drew a deep breath, and dove.

Kicking hard, she had propelled herself deep under the water. She still had her eyes closed—her natural response, which was dumb. She had to open them.

Don't think—just do it, she had thought.

Everything had been blurry, and the murky water disoriented her. Sarah had found the pressure on her eyes discomforting, but she kept kicking with determination. Finally Sarah had seen a glint of light reflect near the bottom. Time had been growing short. Her lungs had burned, protesting the lack of air, and her heart pounded. She had felt lightheaded but kicked even harder toward the bottom. However, the reflection had not gotten any closer. Sarah had turned toward the surface, and to her dismay it was far away. The water pressed upon her, her lungs screamed, and she fought the urge to open her mouth, knowing she would drown. Somehow, someway, she kicked for the surface, leaving the ladle behind. Air was what she had needed. Breaking the surface of the water, Sarah had gasped for breath and gulped in the precious air. That had been when she heard it.

Laughter.

Her vision cleared and she had seen the other girls laughing and pointing at her. She did not understand until she spied Mary standing on shore still holding the ladle in her hand. She had thrown a rock and sent Sarah on a wild goose chase. One that she had almost not come back from.

Of all Sarah's memories, this was the one she relived as the tunnel collapsed around her. She was convinced she was nearing the end of her time on earth. Just before reaching the tunnel's end, everything had come crushing in around her for some unknown reason. She screamed, squeezed her eyes shut, and held her breath—waiting for it to be over. Sarah felt like she was being pushed forward. Muffled music filled her head and a thumping pulsed through her body.

This was not what she thought the end would be like.

As the thumping grew louder, she felt it in her bones as well as the pressure pushing her body forward. Both feelings grew in intensity. Abruptly, she stopped against some kind of barrier—pressure building behind her. She was being crushed against a wall. The thumping was coming from the other side.

The pressure and crushing pain peaked, then suddenly the wall gave way. Sarah spewed forth, propelled from the tunnel's tomb. She covered her ears in an attempt to dampen the deafening noise now ringing and throbbing in her head. Opening her eyes, she wondered if she were outside—it was dark and she saw stars.

To her left, she spied a platform. She scrambled toward it as best she could. She felt unbalanced, but kept her hands clamped over her ears. Images caught the corner of her vision—a full moon, a railing, shimmering—was that water? The relentless pounding made it difficult to focus. The noise overwhelmed her, reaching inside her brain. Tears ran from her eyes and up ahead she saw a wall of sticks and branches—no not sticks...levers?

Where was she?

Reaching the levers, all she could think of was making the noise stop. Perhaps the levers had something to do with what was making the noise. Keeping one hand over her ear, she used the other to grab the levers. At first she thought it had worked, the sounds quieted. Then she realized the sounds were not stopping, just changing. New sounds blasted and the stars above her started to spin. Blackness overtook her, the sound faded, and she passed out.

THE INVERTED CAVERN

Aaron gripped the arms of the Amish boy to steady himself. Saving him from the fall, the Amish boy held him in an embrace that reminded Aaron of two middle school kids about to dance. They both burst into laughter.

"That was close!" Aaron yelled over the tones. Relaxing his grip, Aaron felt the change. The air in the cavern shifted direction. Some vents along the shore closed while others opened.

"Oh no!"

The cavern quaked. The star field spun, and the moon sped off the horizon, blanketing them in the darkness. A new star locked into place, which Aaron did not recognize. What he did know was that they were too close to the center. Suddenly the time vortex appeared. As Aaron picked up his crutch, the Amish boy yelled, and Aaron gripped his forearm with his free hand.

The force of the time field pulled at them. Aaron anchored the crutch as best he could in the water, holding on to the Amish boy whose legs stretched airborne toward the hungry portal.

"Hold on!" Aaron yelled, seeing the terrified look on the boy's face. "I won't let go. If you go, we both go!"

Samuel's body ejected from the tunnel. Without pausing he shot forward with only one thought—to save Sarah. He questioned nothing, reacting only on instinct. Somewhere in his brain he already accepted that he was dead and had entered some strange afterworld. But he could still move, see, hear, and therefore would find her. His senses heightened and images, sounds, and even smells sharpened into focus. He ran toward the brilliant light below.

Then he saw the boys.

They were struggling, maybe fighting. One was trying to push the other into a brilliant light. No wait, not pushing. Someone inside the light had a hold of one boy. It tugged at him, and the boy was trying to escape.

Sarah!

It had to be her. She must have been pushed into the light, but she had grabbed one of the boys. Now she was trying to escape, but the boys were keeping her away! They were trying to send her into the light forever. He only had a little time. The one boy seemed to be gaining a foothold on something. His mind told him the boys were standing on water, but that made no sense. He needed to move, to get his sister, to save Sarah. What would come then, he did not know.

Chapter 33

NO ADMITTANCE

I think I'm getting used to this, Jake thought as the world materialized around her.

The tree was the same in every time she visited, the only difference had been the addition of the garden hose in her time. Otherwise, the tree, bushes, and other plants were always the same—same size, same shape. It was as if their growth had been permanently suspended. While that should have been familiar and comforting, Jake found it annoying as there was no way for her to know *what* time period she was in.

Arriving in this time she found another change—the tree was open. That was odd. Someone must have gone in. Was it Aaron? Was he trying to get back home? Maybe he and the Amish boy were in there right now. If they were using the moon setting, she would not be in the future to open the portal and let him out. Then again, she already tried that but it did not work. Aaron had not been there.

But something tickled at the back of Jake's brain.

The Amish boy.

He had gone into the moon setting and gotten trapped. She and

Aaron released him by opening the portal in the future. Argh, what was she missing? The answer was forming, she could feel it, but her brain couldn't quite figure it out. It was like trying to remember a blocked word that was on the tip of her tongue. She was on the edge of understanding something important—something key.

It will probably come to me in the middle of the night, she thought. That was when most of her stuck thoughts broke loose. *Until then, I might as well see who is inside the tree.*

As Jake entered the helium room, the tunnel to the cavern was closing.

Weird.

Jake went to the wall and touched the helium symbol. Unlike previous trips, the etched glyph remained motionless.

Odd.

To her left, she noticed the cubby holes filled with helium canisters. She examined one and shook her head. *I bet Aaron flipped when he saw these. Talk about making life a lot easier!*

Deciding not to use the limited number she had brought along, she took a canister from the cubby and connected it to the small nub near the symbol.

A Perfect fit!

"Here goes," she said, squeezing its contents. She stood back and waited for the light to appear and the electrons to spin around the growing nucleus. But nothing happened.

She pulled the tube from the wall, squeezed the canister, and tested its contents.

A twinge of panic struck. If she could not get into the cavern, she could not get home. Opening her backpack, she tested one of her own bottles.

Nothing happened. Nothing at all.

Chapter 34

CHAOS

Sarah opened her eyes and felt the incessant pounding once more throughout her body.

Why won't it stop?

She looked at the levers she had pulled—what were they? What was this place? She stopped and took a good look at everything. That was when she noticed someone running below her.

Could it be? Samuel?

It was him. *But how did he get here?*

Her eyes followed his progress. Leaning over the platform's edge, she saw what could only be described as a whirlpool sucking everything down in a swirling vortex. Some sort of light sprang from the middle of the turbulent water, and her friend fought to free himself.

She screamed but could not hear herself over the pounding. Another boy was there. He was trying to keep Aaron from being sucked in, but it was a losing effort. They were both being pulled forward.

Samuel had reached the edge of the pool. He hesitated and then she realized why. The boys seemed to be standing on top of the water! How was that possible? She did not know and yet she saw it with her own eyes.

"Help them!" she screamed, but it was impossible for her brother to hear her over the deafening noise. She had to do something. Then she remembered the levers.

Maybe they could help.

The boys slipped closer to the vortex as Samuel vaulted toward them. She did not think he would make it. The other boy was losing his grip on the stick he was using. No time left. She had to do something. She pulled a lever, grabbed at others, pushing and pulling wildly.

This is it, Aaron thought, feeling the crutch giving way as his grip slipped. He felt them sliding toward the vortex. His forearm ached from the Amish boy's grip. Aaron tried to pull him without success. Water was everywhere, on his clothes, in his face. He spit out a mouthful and shook his head to clear his sight. His eyes locked with the boy's. He saw his own fear reflected in the boy's face but there was something else— friendship, respect, and finally resignation. The boy was giving up.

"Nooo!" Aaron screamed.

The boy peered over his shoulder at his awaiting fate. Looking back at Aaron, he shook his head.

"Don't give up!" Aaron protested.

The boy smiled sadly as his grip relaxed. He was sacrificing himself.

"I don't think so," Aaron replied, letting go of the crutch and latching on to the boy's arm with both hands. Confusion spread across his friend's face.

The cavern winds shifted. The star field spun again and the boy was propelled free of the vortex. Aaron fell on something, and his friend landed on top of him. There was a splash and undecipherable yelling. A new vortex appeared as another star locked in place. The Amish boy was struggling. For a moment, Aaron thought he was being pulled back in until he saw another boy.

It was Samuel! He had pulled the younger boy off of Aaron and the two struggled. There was pushing, and the Amish boy fell even as Samuel's forward momentum flipped him over and into the vortex.

Samuel disappeared into the time field and the vortex collapsed.

The vents closed, the pounding chorus quieted, the stars faded—

All that remained was an echoing scream.

Jake drummed her fingers on the wall in boredom. She was about to give up and exit the tree when the helium symbol came to life. She swept her hand over it; the electrons glowed and began to spin.

This is so odd.

She fitted the canister tube to the wall and squeezed.

It worked. The atom expanded and the tunnel opened.

Finally!

Halfway down the tunnel, she heard screaming, and broke into a run. Whoever it was, they sounded hysterical. Entering the cavern, Jake did not know what to make of what she saw. Limping up the side pathway were two Amish boys, one with a broken leg leaning on the other for support. On the platform a young Amish girl stood. She was frantically pushing and pulling levers, screaming and crying, then slumped to the floor.

Jake's instincts drew her to the girl, and she folded her arms around her. The girl was startled but did not pull away. Whatever fight she had was now gone.

"Samuel...Samuel...Samuel," she kept repeating.

"What?" Jake replied. She had no idea what was happening. "Who is Samuel?"

"He is gone. It took him." The girl pointed. Then anger flared in her eyes. "It's all their fault!" she screamed at the two boys. "They did this to him."

Jake turned.

"They lost him," the girl continued. "I told him never to come back here. I knew something like this would happen. I tried to stop them. I should have told Samuel the truth from the beginning. I should never have listened to the lies!"

Jake could not see the boys' faces. Their heads were bowed in concentration as they hobbled up the path, and their hats were in the way. When they reached the top, Jake gasped.

"Jake?" Aaron's thoughts reeled. *It's over*, he thought. *With Jake here there's no one left in the future to open the moon setting.* He would be trapped here forever. There would be no going back—for either of them.

"What have I done?"

Chapter 35

ANSWERS

Entering the schoolhouse, Aaron collapsed on the first bench. The girl named Sarah was still upset. As much as he had wanted to talk with Jake and understand why she had followed him, Sarah's condition had kept them preoccupied. Leaving through the tunnel had sent the girl even further over the edge. Screaming in terror and mumbling about drowning, she cowered from the tunnel like a frightened animal.

He had no idea how she or Samuel had gotten to the cavern. As always, it sealed once the water started flowing. So many questions. Questions he was sure the Amish boy had as well but they had agreed to wait until they could regroup at the schoolhouse. They put all their effort into getting there as quickly as possible and trying to calm Sarah who continued to cry, shake, and even let out a wail from time to time.

Jake held the girl's hand, and the Amish boy stroked her hair. It took some time, but eventually she started to calm down. Aaron could not hear much of what had been said but Jake left her side and came over to Aaron.

"She doesn't want me anywhere near her," she said. "It is our fault she says...about her brother."

"Samuel."

"Right," Jake replied. "How did you know?"

"He's been after me ever since I got here. He destroyed the tree's gears then stole the broken ones from us. It's a miracle we could make replacements with nothing to go by."

Jake stared at him but said nothing. Aaron suspected she was holding something back.

"What?" Aaron prompted.

"I'm not sure it was Samuel that did that," Jake suggested while taking a seat beside him.

"Jake, really," he dismissed, "I was here, and saw it all. Well most of it anyway. I saw Samuel steal our stuff. He was in the forest from the minute I arrived."

Jake shook her head a little.

"Honestly Jake, you just got here. How could you know? Speaking of which, what are you doing here?" Aaron struggled to control the frustration, disappointment, and anger he felt. "You know we are trapped," he added. "The moon setting doesn't work here. I couldn't get back and now we are both stuck here."

Shock spread across her face. "The cavern doesn't work!" She covered her mouth as if speaking a bad word.

"No, no I didn't say the cavern doesn't work. I said the moon setting doesn't work. Every other star is just fine. It's only the moon setting that's the problem. All we can do now is travel farther back in time. We're trapped."

Aaron watched the information register on Jake's face. Clearly she understood what he was saying.

"You say the cavern still works, yes?"

"Yeah, but Jake the moon setting…"

"Right, right I got that. We do need the moon setting to get home but not the way you think."

Aaron stared, puzzled.

"I've been to the future, Aaron," she said with a consoling touch of his arm. "My future, your future…four years from our time. I think the moon setting is for traveling forward, but not how we originally thought." Thinking back, Jake remembered the panic of being trapped in the inverted cavern. "The thing is, I went to the moon setting looking for you and I got trapped. I'm still not sure how, so I had to try something crazy and going into the future was all I could come up with. I found a note from myself. A note I hadn't even written—"

"Jake, Jake," Aaron interrupted. "I'm losing you. I don't know what you are talking about. Slow down."

Jake took a breath and fidgeted with her hair, working out her thoughts. "Aaron there's another cavern…"

"What!"

"I tried," Jake explained. "I wanted to follow the plan but right away things went wrong. The diary—"

"Do you have it? I couldn't find it. You were right. I'm sure it can help. What happened? Can I see it?"

"Argh! Too many questions. Just listen for a minute!"

"Sorry."

Jake collected herself. "When you ran into the cavern from the platform, the diary somehow came out of your backpack. I tried to stop you but it was too late."

Aaron thought about his acrobatic leap. "Yeah, not too smart on my part," he admitted. "That's how I broke my leg. I landed badly after reappearing when I went through the vortex. At least I think that is what happened. But the diary—"

"Right," Jake interrupted. "It fell into the water. The pages, got soaked, most of it is unreadable."

For once, Aaron was stunned into silence.

"I was able to salvage some of them, and they helped me find the other cavern but the rest…let's just say if it has the answers, they'll be very hard to find now. I did what I could." Jake went on to explain the process she had used in her attempt to save the book. Aaron could tell how hard she worked to try to recover them. He also sensed how afraid she had been.

"Aaron, I didn't know what happened to you. You never came out of the moon setting. I tried leaving the cavern open but kept running out of water. Eventually, I had to change plans. I had to look for you." She stopped and her cheeks reddened.

Was she embarrassed?

She continued, "I thought maybe you were hurt. After almost getting trapped myself, I figured out how to rig a hose to feed water from the stream. It should have kept the portal open indefinitely."

Jake explained the contraption and Aaron was impressed with her ingenuity. It was a great idea—amazing in fact. When she explained the inverted cavern he could hardly believe it. It made sense though that there would be a more straightforward way for journeying forward in time versus relying on someone from the future.

"Wow," Aaron said. "I can't believe you actually went into the light column. How did you know it would work?"

"I didn't," she countered. "But I didn't have a choice. I was trapped. It was the only way out."

"Trapped? How? I thought you had rigged the hose contraption."

"I did," she explained, rising from the bench. "At first, I thought it was because I messed with the controls."

Aaron frowned. "You said 'at first.' Now, you don't think so?"

"No," she said. "I think I know what happened and it wasn't my doing."

Aaron waited for the explanation but none came. "Well, what is it?"

Jake fidgeted. "Aaron, when I got back to our time, I found that someone had taken the hose out of the stream."

Aaron's eyes widened and he lifted one eyebrow. "What are you saying Jake?"

"I'm saying someone else knows about the cavern, and they purposely took the hose out of the stream." Jake jabbed in the air as she spoke. "And I think that is what eventually closed the exit to the inverted cavern. The good news is, unlike the other cavern, water apparently isn't needed to make the inverted cavern work—it just controls the entrance."

Someone else knew? Was it the same person who drew the map in the sand for the Amish boy? What about the person who called his name on the wind? Was this person following them through time?

"Any idea who it might be?"

Jake stared off. "I don't know. The only people who know about the cavern are you, me, the Amish boy, and Sarah."

"And Samuel…"

"What?"

"Samuel, Sarah's brother, he knows. He tried destroying the cavern and stole the gears. He knows."

"Yes and no." A new voice entered their conversation. Jake and Aaron turned to see the Amish boy join them.

"What do you mean?" Aaron asked.

The boy leaned against the wall one leg on the bench. "Well, 'yes,' because Samuel knows about the cavern, but I think today was his first time there. Sarah never showed it to him, and since we didn't either, I suspect he must have followed his sister. And 'no' because he didn't destroy the gears—"

"Of course he did! He broke them into a million pieces then stole them!" Aaron interrupted.

"No, it was Sarah," the boy said, then paused. "She was the one who smashed everything." He glanced back toward her. Sarah had her head buried in her hands, her shoulders shaking as she wept. "After I disappeared she barely held it together, which is why she confided in Samuel. When we asked her to try to trick him, to make him think it was just a game, she realized he would continue poking around and would eventually find the cavern. She thought we were playing around with something we didn't understand. She knew we would try to use the cavern to send you home, and messing with it could be dangerous. She wanted us to just leave it alone, but she knew we wouldn't."

Aaron shrugged sheepishly.

"Samuel had found your flashlight. When Sarah saw him with it, she knew it had come from the future. It was then that she decided to destroy it—and the tree."

Aaron looked over at the girl but glanced away when she caught his eye.

The boy continued. "She wanted her world to go back to the way it had been."

Aaron shook his head. "She was right."

Jake and the Amish boy looked at him in stunned silence.

Aaron explained. "Look at what has happened. Samuel is gone… the moon setting doesn't work…we had no idea what we were doing."

"But we can get him," the boy protested. "We can go to whatever time he was sent to."

Aaron massaged his forehead.

"I don't think so," Jake answered before he could speak.

"Why?" the boy asked.

"When I came into the chamber," Jake explained. "Sarah was

frantically pulling the levers—after the cavern shut down."

Aaron nodded almost imperceptibly and the boy frowned.

"She moved the levers?" the boy whispered.

"Exactly," Jake said.

"Unless you know which star was targeted when he went in…" Aaron trailed off.

The Amish boy hung his head. "He could be anywhere…"

Silence. Even Sarah's sobs had stopped.

"The missing boy…" Aaron whispered.

"What?" Jake asked.

"Well something's always bothered me about sending our young Amish friend back in time…he made it home. He is here. He isn't missing. Yet, there was the legend of the missing Amish boy. Remember, Jake, you told me about it when I first moved here—how my house was haunted. We thought the missing boy was Aaron here—which he was, but when we sent him back, history should have changed. He was no longer missing so there wouldn't have been a legend, and you wouldn't have told me about it. But Samuel is missing…maybe forever. Maybe the legend is about him."

Sarah overheard and gasped, and the Amish boy grimaced.

"I don't know, Aaron. That doesn't make sense to me," Jake whispered.

"I guess it's hard to know," Aaron said. "Either history is playing out exactly as it should, or we changed it."

"I guess I'll trust you on that point," Jake added. "It's just… shouldn't the Amish Aaron be stuck in the moon setting right at this moment, waiting for us to release him in the future? How can he be here too?"

Aaron grabbed her by the shoulders. "Jake, that's it!"

Jake and the Amish boy looked wide eyed at one another.

"That's why the moon setting doesn't work! Remember what you told us?" Aaron asked the Amish boy. "Time passed almost instantaneously for you when in the moon setting. One moment the portal closed, the next it opened. You climbed out but it was one hundred years later."

The boy nodded, and Jake shrugged.

Aaron smacked his head. "How stupid can I be? Of course I couldn't enter the moon setting…it was already 'in use.'" He pointed to the Amish boy. "You were there…or are there."

Jake pursed her lips and furrowed her eyebrows.

"Don't you see? When we opened the cavern in the future, it collapsed your time and our time to the same point. Nothing in between exists."

"Okaaay…" Jake grimaced. "What does this mean?"

"The time we are in now—it's the in-between. It means the moon setting won't work. It's like it's locked in a way. The moon setting should work anytime before he entered and anytime after we opened the cavern."

Jake's eyes lit up. "It did! That's how I was able to find the inverted cavern." Then her shoulders slumped. "Of course, we need the moon setting to get home even for the inverted cavern. And if this is in-between time, we're stuck here!"

Aaron gave her a big smile.

"Jake, we can get to the moon setting! You got to it in the future *after* we pulled him out. Now all we have to do is go into the moon setting *before* he went in." Aaron watched Jake as the realization hit her. She snorted a laugh and slugged the Amish boy in the shoulder.

"What?" he asked. "What am I missing?"

"All Aaron and I have to do is go back in time, to a time before you went into the cavern. Then the moon setting will work." A smug smile spread across her face. She stood with her shoulders back, head held high, confident, forceful but not overbearing. "I'd suggest four years," she added.

"Why four?" Aaron questioned.

"Let's just say I've got the star for a four-year journey memorized."

"I can't wait to hear about that," he said, grabbing his crutch and standing up.

"Well I can tell some of it but not all. Because,"—she winked—"it's best not to know too much about the past, or the future. We don't want to mess anything up."

Yup he thought. *Something is definitely different.* And Aaron smiled.

Chapter 36

BACK AND FORTH

They went straight from the schoolhouse to the cavern. The Amish Aaron came too, but Sarah was nowhere to be found.

"I'll check on her later," the Amish boy said. "She probably ran home."

Aaron glanced quickly at Jake.

"Don't worry, Aaron," the boy added. "I will make sure she doesn't say anything to anyone, or try to destroy the tree again." He adjusted the platform levers to Jake's specifications. "By the way, what will you do if this doesn't work?"

"If the moon setting doesn't work there, then we'll have to find a different answer," he explained. "If it does, then we'll check out Jake's new inverted cavern."

The boy furrowed his brow, and pulled his earlobe. "That doesn't seem like much of a plan."

Jake engaged the main lever, turned sharply, and grabbed Aaron's arm. "It'll work."

BACK AND FORTH

ॐ

Aaron breathed a sigh of relief as they both materialized. They walked in silence to the tree, wondering if they had gone back four years.

When they arrived at the tree, the pit in Aaron's stomach grew. "Okay, let's get it over with," he said.

Jake grasped the notch.

"Well?" he asked, and Jake responded with a large grin.

"Come take a look!"

Sun glinted off the pristine gears. They were perfect—and all metal.

It worked!

He did not know if they had gone back four years or forty thousand. But it did not matter. If he and Jake were right, the moon setting should work.

"You're wondering what year it is, aren't you?" Jake asked as they entered the tree.

"Actually, I was. How did you know?"

"I did the same thing when I went to the future. The only way I knew for sure was when I…" She paused, thinking about his house, his desk, the picture.

"What aren't you telling me?"

"It's nothing, Aaron. Nothing bad. I was only there for a little while and didn't see much."

Aaron considered her hesitation. "No, you're right not to tell me. I shouldn't know." He wondered if she could sense his frustration. Everything felt topsy-turvy. Jake was the one to come back and save the day and she had most, if not all, of the answers. How had she found the inverted cavern and gone to the future? Jake? She had always been afraid. Now…

"So weren't you scared?"

"Scared of what?" Jake asked.

"You know, about going to the future, of getting trapped, all of that? How did you do it?"

Jake shook her head. "I guess I couldn't stop searching until I found you." She blushed, and he saw a flicker of surprise in her eyes, as if she had not realized the answer until she said it. "But, yeah, I was afraid, especially when I thought I was trapped inside the inverted cavern. Oh and the time I almost got trapped in the moon setting. But I couldn't give up. Sometimes you do what you have to—especially when others need you." She laughed.

"What?"

"I think I just sounded like my mom."

Aaron chuckled. Parents were funny that way. They try to turn everything into what his dad called "teachable moments." Aaron honestly thought he had tuned them out, but occasionally he found himself parroting back stuff his parents had said. Apparently, Jake had a similar affliction. *Argh!* he thought, *parents can be tricky.*

"I wonder how far back in time we can actually go." Jake commented. "I mean, stars go back to just after the big bang—would the cavern let us go back that far? And if so, where would we reappear? The earth wouldn't even exist, much less the tree."

"I don't know," he answered. What a terrifying possibility that raised. Was there a time they could go back to where the tree did not exist? He shuddered.

Entering the helium room, Jake grabbed one of the many bottles out of its cubby. "Ah, Aaron…"

"Yeah?"

She turned the bottle over and removed a folded piece of paper taped to the bottom. The words *Jake and Aaron* were written in careful script.

Aaron raised his eyebrows. "You've got to be kidding"

"You know whose writing this is, right?" Jake asked.

Aaron nodded. It was the Amish boy. How the heck did it get here? Were they in the past?

"Guess we should open it."

She unfolded the note, the paper seemed crisp and new.

Jake and Aaron,

Sarah is gone!

After you left, I went home and found my room had been messed with and the diary was open on the floor. It had to have been Sarah. She was terrified for Samuel and blamed herself. I looked for her at her farm and the schoolhouse, but she was nowhere to be found.

I had a feeling her guilt over Samuel had driven her to make a rash decision. I feared the worst and ran to the tree. Inside, I found another helium bottle had been used and thrown off to the corner of the room.

I hid the remaining bottles, and knew I had to find her.

In the cavern, I found the levers targeting a star I did not recognize. I have drawn a picture of their settings below. I am going after her. I do not know if it is even my place to ask after what you have been through, but if you are willing I need your help. I do not think I can do this alone.

Aaron folded the note and opened his backpack.

"What are you doing?"

"We've got to find them!"

"I know that," Jake said, grabbing the note. "But give that to me. We don't want a repeat of the diary incident. I'll keep it safe."

"Fine, let's go home and regroup."

Standing at the control panels in the inverted cavern, Aaron stared, mouth agape. *It is an inverted cavern.* Jake manipulated the controls like a pro and Aaron felt a wave of nausea as the star field spun at her command.

"Where do those other platforms go?" he asked.

"Don't know," Jake said keeping focused on the task at hand.

"And you say the exit from our tree closed at some point."

"Right," she clipped. "I think it closed when the water from the normal cavern stopped and the vortex to the moon setting closed. Had it not been for the drawing and the notes on the diary pages I recovered, I'm not sure I would have put it all together."

"Amazing," he said. "Jake, you did it. It seems obvious now to have checked the tree for a hidden mechanism, but honestly, I never would have thought of it."

She smiled, straightening her shoulders.

"If you are right," he continued, "about the exit being closed off because the tube in the other time cavern ran out of water, that may explain why we can't exit from the other platforms here. They must lead somewhere but their exits are closed from the outside."

Jake lifted her hands from the panel and pointed. "I think we are set. The star is locked in for home."

Aaron checked the constellation confirming her setting. "I still have questions," he added.

Jake nodded. She opened her mouth for a moment, then held back. "Are we ready to go?" he asked.

"One more thing," Jake said. "You got any tape in that backpack?"

"I think so." Aaron fished out a roll and handed it over. "What do you need it for?"

"You'll see."

She tore off a piece of paper and wrote in big letters:

This Way to the Future!

Jake taped it to the control console and walked with him toward the light column.

"What was that about?" he asked.

"Just something I had to do."

Aaron nodded though he was not sure why. Waiting just outside the swirling light he turned to her. "You, my friend, have a lot of explaining to do!"

"Me?" she replied coyly. "Hardly. I'm not the one with the broken leg. I can't imagine how you are going to explain that to your folks!"

Before he could respond, she grabbed his hand and walked into the light.

BOOKS BY TODD FONESCA

AARON & JAKE TIME TRAVEL SERIES

The Time Cavern (The first adventure)

The Inverted Cavern (The second adventure)

About the Author

Todd A. Fonseca grew up in the northern Indiana city of Mishawaka. This small town is home to a large Amish community. Those visiting the area experience the Amish through the town's shops and nearby Amish Acres. Todd learned of the Amish culture through frequent family Sunday drives to rural Nappanee Indiana.

During these early years, Fonseca's interest in the arts began with music. He became an accomplished accordionist participating in national competitions leading to a #4 placement in 1983. Fonseca has also performed in New York's Carnegie Recital Hall. His high school career added drama to his resume. Having the role of curmudgeon Mr. Hassler in The Pajama Game, led to being cast as the lead in the production Jack and the Beanstalk.

The Time Cavern is his first published work, and was a finalist for the 2009 National Indie Excellence Award for Young Adult Fiction. His second book, Inverted: The Second Adventure was released in November 2011.

At Marquette University, Fonseca received a Biomedical Engineering graduate degree. His professional career includes numerous positions in medical device companies. He is currently a senior clinical research director for a company researching deep brain stimulation for treating conditions such as Parkinson's Disease. Fonseca lives in Minnesota with his wife and four boys.

Contact

Website: www.thetimecavern.com

Email: ridan.publishing@gmail.com - to contact Todd, or register to be notified of future releases